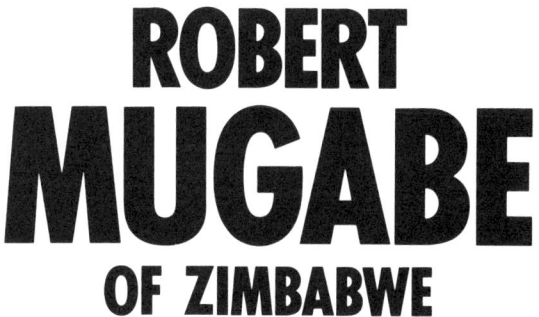

IN FOCUS BIOGRAPHIES

ROBERT MUGABE OF ZIMBABWE
BY RICHARD WORTH

MARGARET THATCHER OF GREAT BRITAIN
BY MARIETTA D. MOSKIN

IN FOCUS

ROBERT MUGABE OF ZIMBABWE

RICHARD WORTH

JULIAN MESSNER

TWIN VALLEY MIDDLE SCHOOL
LIBRARY MEDIA CENTER

Copyright © 1990 by Richard Worth
All rights reserved including the right of
reproduction in whole or in part in any form.
Published by Julian Messner, a division of
Silver Burdett Press, Inc., Simon & Schuster, Inc.
Prentice Hall Bldg., Englewood Cliffs, NJ 07632

JULIAN MESSNER and colophon are trademarks of
Simon & Schuster, Inc. Design by Leslie Bauman
Manufactured in the United States of America.

Lib. ed.   10 9 8 7 6 5 4 3 2 1
Paper ed. 10 9 8 7 6 5 4 3 2 1

Library of Congress Cataloging-in-Publication Data

Worth, Richard
Robert Mugabe of Zimbabwe/Richard Worth.
p.   cm.—(In focus biographies)
Includes bibliographical references.
Summary: Recounts the story of the man who led the struggle for black political power in the emerging nation of Zimbabwe and was elected its first prime minister.
1. Mugabe, Robert Gabriel, 1924- —Juvenile literature.
2. Prime ministers—Zimbabwe—Biography—Juvenile literature.
[1. Mugabe, Robert Gabriel, 1924-   2. Prime ministers.]
3. Zimbabwe—Politics and government.]   I. Title.   II. Series.
DT3000.M28W67   1990
968.9105′092—dc20
[B]
[92]   90-31492
ISBN 0-671-68987-8 LSB   CIP
ISBN 0-671-70684-5 paper   AC

CONTENTS

PREFACE vii
1 BEGINNINGS 11
2 THE STRUGGLE FOR FREEDOM 30
3 A NEW NATION AND A NEW LEADER 39
4 ZIMBABWE—A SNAPSHOT 52
5 A BLACK AND WHITE ECONOMY 61
6 SERVICES FOR ALL THE PEOPLE 70
7 PRESERVING WILDLIFE 81
8 POLITICS IN ZIMBABWE 86
TIME LINE 97
GLOSSARY 99
BIBLIOGRAPHY 105
INDEX 108

PREFACE

This book tells two stories, woven closely together. One is the story of Robert Mugabe, president of Zimbabwe. The other is the history of Zimbabwe, a country of approximately ten million people located in southern Africa. Both make fascinating subjects because they are so complex and so full of contradictions.

Many have called Robert Mugabe a national hero. Yet others see him as a cold-blooded opportunist who is only interested in power. Before coming to power, Mugabe spent almost twenty years waging war against a white minority that used to run Zimbabwe (formerly called Southern Rhodesia). Today he works closely with whites who praise him for his policies. As a devoted Marxist, Mugabe believes in government control of the economy. Yet he governs a country whose economy is based on private enterprise. As president Mugabe has worked tirelessly to improve the lives of Zimbabweans through education and public health programs. Yet he has also taken many lives in a brutal effort to silence his political foes.

Robert Mugabe is a very complex and contradictory man. But in this he is no different from Zimbabwe. The spacious capital of Harare is one of Africa's most modern cities. But only a short distance beyond the city limits, the people still live in mud huts with no electricity or running water. A majority of Zimbabwe's people are Christian. Yet they continue to worship their ancestors and pray to tribal gods for bountiful harvests. While some Zimbabwean women campaign tirelessly for equal rights, many others seem content to continue to work hard for little pay and no recognition.

In each of these areas Zimbabwe may be much like many other African nations. But there are also critical differences. On a continent where most countries cannot grow enough food to feed their people, Zimbabwe grows more than enough for all. And, unlike many other African countries, industry in Zimbabwe is flourishing, helped by communications and transportation systems that work efficiently. In addition to these pluses, the nation is rich in natural resources.

Today Zimbabwe is considered the most successful country in black Africa and Robert Mugabe its most effective political leader. In a part of the world beset by starvation, poverty, and disappointment, Zimbabwe is a symbol of hope—the hope of a better future.

ROBERT MUGABE
OF ZIMBABWE

CHAPTER 1

BEGINNINGS

It was December—summer in Southern Rhodesia—when the welcome rains come to soak the dry landscape. A large crowd of Africans had gathered for a political rally in Salisbury, the nation's capital, to press their demands for power against a repressive white minority government that had ruled them for almost seventy years. Now they watched as an intense, bespectacled man of medium height and strong build stepped forward to speak. In the weeks leading up to the rally, he had called upon his supporters to practice self-denial as a way of dramatizing their political struggle. He had also urged them to reject all European traditions and practice only African customs. One of these customs was taking off their shoes at political meetings, as they did on this day.

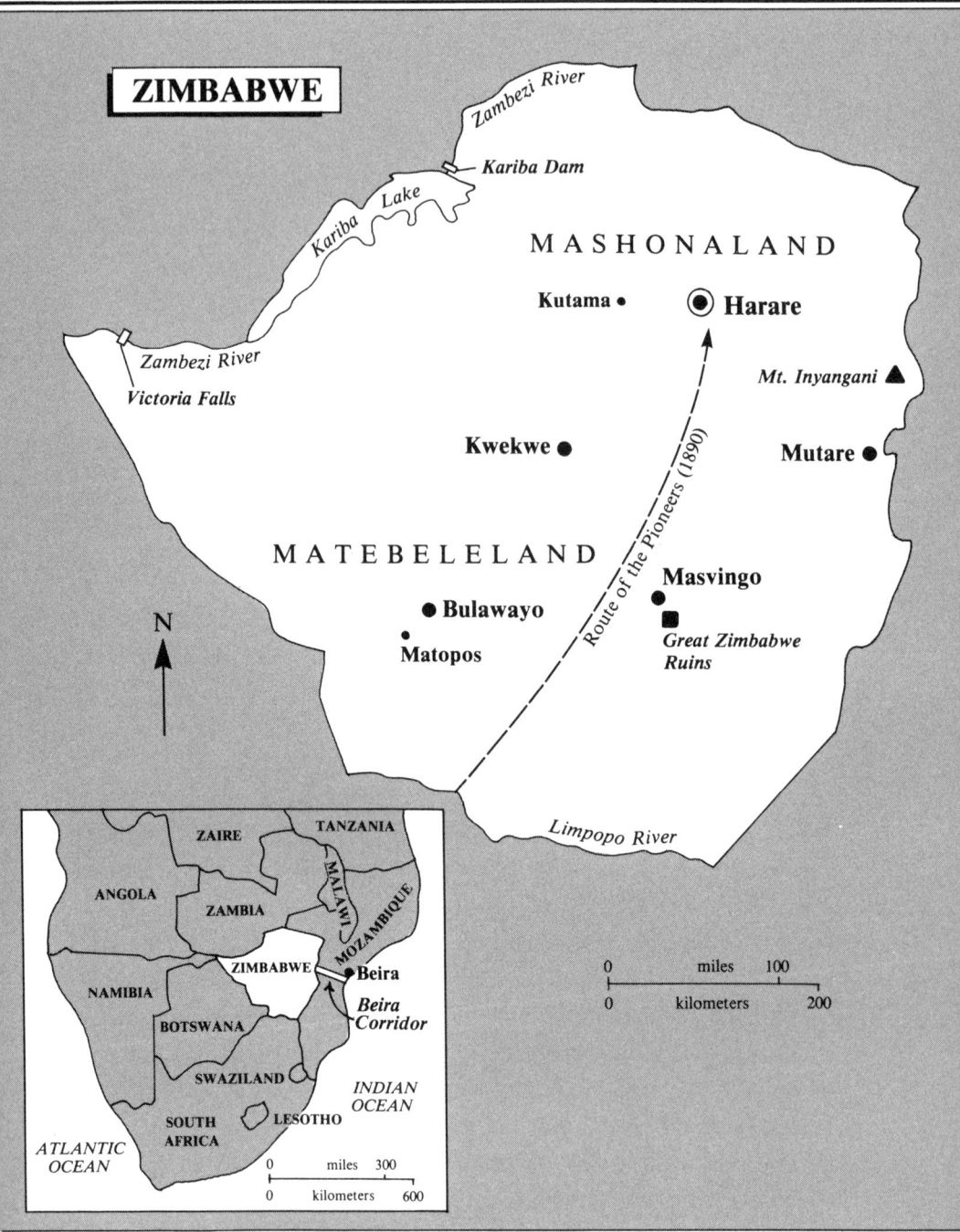

While the crowd of more than 20,000 listened, he told them: "Today you removed your shoes. Tomorrow you may be called upon to destroy them altogether, or to perform other acts of self-denial. If European industries are used to buy guns which are aimed against us, we must...destroy those industries."[1]

As Robert Gabriel Mugabe addressed the Salisbury gathering in 1961, the struggle for black political power in Southern Rhodesia was just beginning. It would take almost twenty years to complete. But when the new nation of Zimbabwe was finally established, Mugabe would be hailed as one of its founders. He would also be elected its first prime minister.

This is the story of the birth of a nation, the rise to power of its political leader, and a close look at the way that nation is being governed today.

SHONA AND NDEBELE

The word *zimbabwe* has roots that run deep in African culture. It was almost a thousand years ago that the Shonas, the largest ethnic group in the region (and the one to which Mugabe belongs), began to build the royal city of Great Zimbabwe in southern Africa. At its zenith the city may have housed up to 20,000 people. Their clay huts were enclosed by massive walls, in which all the stones were fitted together without the use of mortar. In fact, *zimbabwe* means "stone enclosure," and the stout walls of Great Zimbabwe may have served as a defense against the Shona's enemies.

Great Zimbabwe was the home of the Shona's royal court and their priest-king. The city contained lavish palaces, well-stocked markets, and numerous religious shrines. Outside the walls large herds of cattle grazed, and the fields yielded plentiful harvests that fed the entire population. But while agriculture was an important occupation of the city's people, it was principally trade that made Great Zimbabwe famous. The city was located near rich deposits of gold and other metals, and the Shona traded in gold as well as ivory and cotton cloth.

The Shonas of ancient Zimbabwe created several stone fortresses centuries before the arrival of the Europeans. In this picture of the ruins of Great Zimbabwe, you can see how the builders used stones to create massive walls and cone-shaped towers, all without the use of mortar.

After a number of centuries Great Zimbabwe began to decline. It was finally abandoned by the Shona kings about 1450. Perhaps the fields grew less fertile from repeated plantings and could no longer provide enough food for the population. As Great Zimbabwe fell on difficult times, the Shona broke up into smaller kingdoms. These survived for almost four hundred years. But eventually, in the early 1800s many of them were conquered by the Ndebele, an ethnic group of battle-hardened warriors who invaded from the south.

The victory of the Ndebele, however, was to be very short-lived, for they soon faced a far more powerful enemy—the English from the Cape Colony on the southern tip of Africa. The British invasion of the Ndebele territory was part of the mad scramble for Africa that occurred in the late 1800s. European nations—England, France, Germany, Belgium—gobbled up huge chunks of the continent and turned them into colonies, all in the name of imperialism. Cecil Rhodes, for example, who launched the English attack against the Ndebele, dreamed of building an enormous British empire in Africa. It would stretch from Cape Town in the southern Cape Colony north to Cairo in Egypt. But Rhodes was also inspired by another motive: greed. He had come to Kimberley in the Cape Colony as a young man and had grown fabulously rich in the gold mines and the diamond fields there. He strongly believed there might be greater riches to the north.

After intense negotiations the British eventually tricked the Ndebele chief, Lobengula, into signing a treaty that would let them send an expedition to Matebeleland (the land of the Ndebele). Armed with this piece of paper, Rhodes organized the so-called Pioneer Column, which included about two hundred settlers and four hundred police from the Cape Colony. In May 1890 the Pioneer Column left Kimberley and snaked northward across the Limpopo River into Matebeleland. Here the British built a string of fortified outposts that would enable them to lay claim to the area and defend it in case of Ndebele attack. Continuing northward, the Pioneer

Cecil John Rhodes during the Ndebele and Shona uprising of 1896. Rhodes made a fortune in southern Africa and colonized the territory that became Rhodesia. In later life he established scholarships.

Column finally completed its journey in September and established a tiny settlement that they called Salisbury. This would later become the capital of a new country named Southern Rhodesia, in honor of Cecil Rhodes.[2]

For the English settlers this first summer in Salisbury turned out to be extremely difficult. It was one of the rainiest summers in memory. Mosquitoes carrying deadly malaria disease buzzed everywhere. Hordes of termites ate through the mud and wooden huts that the settlers had hastily erected. During the next few years the new settlement also had to withstand determined attacks from the

Ndebele and the Shona. Alarmed that the English would take all his lands, Lobengula sent out his young warriors to push them back across the Limpopo in late 1893.

But the fierce Ndebele were simply no match for the British machine guns, which slaughtered them by the hundreds. Nevertheless, the Ndebele rose up again. This time they were joined by the Shona in a general war known as the Chimurenga, fought between 1896 and 1897. But once more the British defeated them. So decisive was the British victory that there were no further uprisings. In the late 1800s the British began to spread their authority over the entire territory of Southern Rhodesia. European settlers were invited to come to the region with promises of good soil and bright prospects for the future. By the early 1900s there were over 10,000 white settlers in Southern Rhodesia.

THE BRITISH TAKE CHARGE

The English not only defeated the Africans on the battlefield, they stripped them of their livelihoods, too. Most of their cattle were taken. Their rich grazing lands were confiscated and given to the white settlers. The British forced many Africans to move to reserves, barren, harsh lands with soil so poor it was nearly impossible to farm. Here they were expected to survive as best they could. The English then demanded that the Shona and Ndebele pay taxes. In order to raise money for the taxes, the Africans had to go to work for the English settlers on their farms and in their mines. Since the British believed that the *Kaffirs*—as they disparagingly called the Africans—were lazy by nature, they reasoned that the hard work would do them good. More importantly the British also obtained a cheap source of labor by keeping wages pitifully low.

Thousands of other Africans eventually became servants in the homes of white settlers or employees in white-owned businesses. Many of these were located in the growing towns of Salisbury or to the south in Bulawayo. These prosperous settlements were inhabited by whites only. Blacks were forced to live in poor townships on the outskirts of the white towns. Most people here resided in tiny one-room shacks. Each day blacks had to travel miles to work in the white communities, and then return home again.

The white government of Southern Rhodesia tried to maintain strict control over the comings and goings of the black population (much as whites in South Africa have done). For the journey back and forth to Salisbury or Bulawayo an African needed to have a pass or risk criminal charges. A special pass was necessary if a black worker had to remain overnight in a white area. And every African was also required to have a certificate of registration showing where he or she lived.

Inside the white towns, blacks were forced to endure all the humiliations of living in a society based on discrimination. In the shops, for example, blacks were served only after whites had been waited on. In the post offices blacks had to use a separate entrance and a separate counter. There were also separate restaurants, separate hospitals, and separate public lavatories for each race. There was discrimination in two other key areas as well. Education throughout Southern Rhodesia was available almost exclusively for whites. And all the political power rested in the hands of the small white minority. The country's parliamentary form of government was run by a prime minister and a legislature elected by the votes of the adult male population. But voting was open only to adults who owned a certain amount of property. Since most blacks owned little or no property, they couldn't qualify to vote.

In a country that was overwhelmingly black, the black African counted for very little. Economically, socially, and politically, Africans were given the status of second-class citizens by the whites. The English believed that the blacks were not capable of governing themselves or even appreciating the benefits of an education. Although this outlook is impossible to justify, it was fairly standard among white Europeans living in Africa during the early 1900s. Some Southern Rhodesians believed that the blacks were simply there to be exploited. Other, more enlightened Rhodesians thought that the blacks might eventually be taught to improve themselves and perhaps some day might even be given a little political power. But that day was still far distant.

ROBERT MUGABE—THE EARLY YEARS

Only 50 miles from Salisbury—the center of white rule—lay the village of Kutama, nestled in the African bush. Here Robert Gabriel Mugabe was born on February 21, 1924. He was one of four children, all of them boys: Michael, the oldest, Robert, Donald, and Sabina.

Robert grew up on a farm and, as a boy, he was responsible for taking care of his family's cattle and keeping them from trampling on the neighbor's crops. If Robert failed in his duties, a neighbor might deliver a reprimand or even spank him. Discipline for every child was the responsibility of all the adults in a village. This enabled children to learn manners and respect.

In Kutama, as in other African villages, traditions are passed down by word of mouth from one generation to the next. An elder would often accompany Robert while he was herding and tell him stories about the great Shona leaders of the past. Robert and the other small boys also learned boxing while they tended the herds. Boxing matches were usually run by some of the older boys who acted as referees to ensure that each match was fought fairly.

When Robert was about ten, his father—a traveling carpenter—abandoned the family to work in Bulawayo and later in the South African mines. The boys were left in the care of their mother, Bona. She was a strong woman who helped instill in Robert habits of hard work and self-reliance.

In many ways Robert was fortunate to live in Kutama, for the village had achieved a notable reputation in Southern Rhodesia as a center of learning. The Jesuits, an order of Roman Catholic priests, had established a mission at Kutama, and also built an elementary school, a teacher training school, and a technical college. Jesuits

NATIONAL ARCHIVES OF ZIMBABWE

Robert Mugabe was born in the village of Kutama in 1924 and attended this school as a young boy. Notice the animal decorations on the walls.

had been in Southern Rhodesia since the days of the earliest European settlers. Along with various Protestant religious groups, they struggled to bring Christianity to the African people. The Christian missionaries also felt it was their responsibility to educate the Africans. And the mission schools provided almost the only formal education available to blacks in Southern Rhodesia.

As a boy Robert attended the Jesuit elementary school. Then, with financial aid from Father Jerome O'Hea, principal of the elementary school, he was able to enter the teacher's training school. Father Jerry O'Hea was Robert's early mentor—someone who recognized the young man's extraordinary intellectual abilities and wanted to see him succeed.

The plucky Jesuit was a strong believer in the equality of the races. One of his goals was to build a hospital at Kutama for blacks, who were without adequate medical facilities. Father O'Hea tried to raise money from the government to build the hospital. But it wasn't going to be easy. The white politicians believed that hospitals, like schools, were unnecessary for blacks. As one white political leader told Father O'Hea: "Why do you worry about hospitals? After all, there are too many natives in the country already." But Father O'Hea did worry. Without any financial aid from Salisbury he finally managed to complete the hospital. It was the only medical facility for blacks in the entire area.

A TEACHER

In 1943 Mugabe left Kutama with a diploma from the teacher training school and began his own career as a teacher at mission schools in Southern Rhodesia. At one of these schools he met Ndabaningi Sithole. Years later both men would become prominent leaders in their nation's struggle for freedom.

Mugabe had taught for only a few years at the missions when he won a scholarship to the all-black university of Fort Hare in South Africa. Here Mugabe studied English and history. He also heard for the first time the fiery speeches of young Nelson Mandela and other leaders of the African National Congress (ANC) who were waging a struggle for political power against the white government of South Africa. Mugabe also began to read the writings of Karl Marx and absorb the principles of communism, which called for world revolution. Another important source of inspiration for him was Mahatma Gandhi. From 1893 to 1914, Gandhi had lived in South Africa and had courageously spoken out against discrimination there before returning home to India and leading his nation's independence movement.

After earning his B.A. degree in 1951, Mugabe returned to Southern Rhodesia, where the struggle for black nationalism was becoming more intense. In 1955 James Chikerema, who had grown up with Mugabe in Kutama, helped form the City Youth League. The next year the league called a massive strike of black workers in Salisbury. The strikers were protesting a fare increase on the buses that Africans rode each day from black townships to their jobs inside the white areas of the city. The league was successful in getting the fares reduced and hailed the strike as a great victory. Eventually the City Youth League merged with another group, the Southern Rhodesian African National Congress. Heading this new organization was Joshua Nkomo, a social worker who had become a labor leader in Bulawayo. While Chikerema wanted to take power from the whites, Nkomo was more moderate and simply wished to share power with them. Nevertheless, he demanded that blacks be given a voice in government immediately. As Nkomo said: "What we are asking for immediately is direct participation in the...government. And we ask...as people who know their rights cannot indefinitely be withheld from them."[3]

Most whites were firmly opposed to Nkomo because he threatened their position in Rhodesian society. Since the end of World War II in 1945, a large number of whites had left battle-scarred Britain and emigrated to Southern Rhodesia, where they hoped to find better lives. The newcomers found jobs that paid more money than they could ever hope to earn at home, taxes were much lower, and they could even afford servants because the wages for domestic help were so low. In fact, it was cheap black labor that supported the entire Southern Rhodesian economy. Rhodesia's two main exports, tobacco and cotton, competed successfully in world markets because they were moderately priced. The reason for this was simple. The cost of producing tobacco and cotton was low because black laborers were paid so little money by white plantation owners.

While the white minority in Rhodesia lived comfortably, the black majority struggled in dire poverty. Nkomo wanted to change the situation and improve the position of blacks. Although many Rhodesians felt threatened by Nkomo's demands, others took a more moderate view. One of these was Garfield Todd, who had been elected prime minister during the 1950s. Todd wanted to grant blacks more political rights, and he even held talks with Nkomo on these issues. But the prime minister had to walk a very thin line between his desire to help the blacks and his need to retain the support of the white voters who had put him into office. So he swung back and forth, supporting blacks on a few issues and then acting tough with them on many others.

Mugabe tells a story about an incident involving Prime Minister Todd that revealed Todd's tough side. The prime minister had decided to cut the salaries of African teachers as a way of reducing the size of the government's budget. Those salaries were already meager, and Mugabe protested to Todd that they should not be cut any further. "He was an excessively domineering man," Mugabe said of Prime Minister Todd. "I told him I would box [hit] him if necessary."

THE MAKING OF A LEADER

During the 1950s the incident involving Prime Minister Todd was almost the only occasion that Mugabe became involved in politics. Most of his time and attention was devoted to furthering his education and to teaching. In 1958 he left Rhodesia to take up a new teaching position in Ghana, a country located in western Africa.

When he arrived in Ghana, the country was on the brink of achieving its independence from Great Britain. The late 1950s marked the beginning of a vast movement sweeping across Africa in which most colonies would win their independence from European nations. In Ghana a charismatic politician named Kwame Nkrumah had become the leader of the government. Nkrumah was trying to attract educated blacks from the entire continent to work in his country and make it a model of African progress.

Robert Mugabe married Sally Hayfron in 1961. Sally is a Ghanaian and, like her husband, a former teacher.

Mugabe was inspired by Nkrumah and exhilarated by all the opportunities available to blacks inside Ghana. For the next three years Mugabe remained in Ghana as a teacher at St. Mary's College. During this time he met Sarah (Sally) Francesca Hayfron, also a teacher at St. Mary's College. Robert Mugabe and Sally Hayfron were married in 1961.

Meanwhile, conditions inside Southern Rhodesia had become more tense. Prime Minister Garfield Todd had been voted out of office by whites who found his policies too moderate. He was replaced by new leaders who took a stronger position against the demands of black nationalists. In 1959 the government banned the Southern Rhodesian African National Congress and imprisoned many of its leaders. Nevertheless, the black nationalist movement continued.

Two prominent nationalists, Michael Mawema and Leopold Takuwera, helped found a new organization in 1960 to carry on the struggle. It was called the National Democratic Party (NDP), and Joshua Nkomo was selected as its leader. Takuwera explained the goals of the NDP this way: "We are no longer asking Europeans to rule us well. We want to rule ourselves."[4]

The NDP had rejected the idea of power sharing and now wanted all the power in the hands of the blacks. When Mugabe returned to Southern Rhodesia in 1960, he talked with Mawema and Takuwera, who urged him to join the movement.

Suddenly, in July, Mawema and Takuwera were arrested by the government. A huge crowd of over 40,000 Africans turned out in the black township of Harare, just outside Salisbury, to protest their arrests. Mugabe joined the protest march. He also delivered a rousing speech to the crowd, calling on people from all classes to join together in the struggle against the white regime.

Mugabe's biographers, David Smith and Colin Simpson, believe the protest march and his speech turned Mugabe into a "committed nationalist." Mugabe saw clearly just how far his country had to progress to achieve what Ghana had already accomplished. But the Rhodesian government had no intention of giving in to the demands of the blacks. Instead, the government arrested many of the blacks who joined the protest marches. Nevertheless, the NDP continued to grow. Moderate Africans who had believed in the possibility of sharing power with whites were convinced by the government's harsh actions that no compromise was possible. They began giving wholehearted support to the NDP.

In October 1960 the party held its first national congress. Robert Mugabe was elected publicity secretary, a leadership position in the NDP. He also began to organize the youth wing of the party, encouraging young people who joined the NDP to wear traditional African dress and reject all European influences.

The day before an NDP rally, members of the youth wing would go door to door urging people to turn out. Mugabe then made sure that the rallies appealed not only to the minds but also to the emotions of the crowds. He enlivened them with African music and dancing, which he believed were important symbols of black nationalism. Mugabe wanted Africans to feel proud of their heritage and to have the courage to challenge the white establishment. As he put it: "Europeans must realize that unless the legitimate demands of African nationalism are recognized, the racial conflict is inevitable."

THE DEEPENING CONFLICT

Thousands of miles away in London the British government looked with growing alarm at the situation in Southern Rhodesia. The British wanted to grant the country its independence, just as they had done in Ghana (1957) and Nigeria (1960) and were about to do in Tanzania (1961) and Zambia (1964). But in every case independence was accompanied by black majority rule. In Southern Rhodesia the white minority of 200,000 did not want to lose control over the black majority of 7,000,000. Britain, however, insisted that independence would be granted only if the whites guaranteed that they would take certain steps toward majority rule.

In 1961, under pressure from Great Britain, the government of Prime Minister Sir Edgar Whitehead did take one small step. A new constitution was passed that enabled blacks to vote for 15 seats in the Southern Rhodesian legislature. Since the whites had 50 seats, however, they would still run the country.

Among black African leaders, the response to the new constitution was mixed. At first Joshua Nkomo hailed it as a great milestone on the road to power. But the other leaders of the NDP, including Mugabe, disagreed. They eventually forced a reluctant Nkomo to change his opinion.

Mugabe then helped organize protests and demonstrations

Joshua Nkomo, left, leader of the NDP, is carried by supporters after the government agreed in 1961 to allow blacks to vote for seats in the Southern Rhodesian legislature.

against the new constitution. In a number of speeches he called on blacks to oppose it. As the campaign against the constitution intensified, riots broke out in Bulawayo and other parts of the country. The government used every means available to control the situation and eventually banned the NDP and arrested some of its leaders.

However, the government's action did not stop the black nationalist movement. The nationalists formed a new organization in 1961, the Zimbabwe African People's Union (ZAPU). They selected Nkomo as its leader. The government retaliated in 1962 by banning

ZAPU and arresting its leaders, including Nkomo and Mugabe. For several months Mugabe was forced to live in a mud hut on a tribal reserve.

After ZAPU's leaders were released, Nkomo wanted his colleagues to leave Southern Rhodesia and move ZAPU headquarters to the safety of Tanzania. Tanzanian president Julius Nyerere supported ZAPU, and Nkomo believed he would give the ZAPU leaders a warm welcome. Instead of risking further arrests at home, they could then carry on the struggle from outside the country.

But Nkomo's plan misfired. From the start it had been strongly opposed by Mugabe and other ZAPU leaders who wanted to stay inside Rhodesia and fight side by side with their followers. Reluctantly they gave in to Nkomo and finally agreed to travel to Tanzania. Once there they found that Nyerere didn't want them. He believed the ZAPU leaders could be much more effective at home.

This incident led directly to a split in ZAPU. For a long time some of its members had been dissatisfied with Nkomo's leadership. In 1963 Mugabe, together with Ndabaningi Sithole and Leopold Takuwera (both of whom had opposed leaving the country) formed a new party. They called it the Zimbabwe African National Union (ZANU). Because of his long service in the nationalist movement, Sithole was selected to lead the organization.

INTO PRISON

While black nationalists were organizing themselves into political parties, the white minority in Southern Rhodesia was growing even more determined to hold out against the demands of the black majority. In elections held during 1962 white voters threw their support to the Rhodesian Front party (RF), which took a determined stand against the African nationalist movement. Led by politicians such as Ian Smith, a member of parliament and a pilot in World War II, the RF hoped to achieve independence under white minority rule.

For Mugabe a return to Southern Rhodesia would mean certain

arrest by the RF government. Nevertheless, he and the other ZANU leaders decided to go home in 1963 to continue the struggle. Once inside the country they were promptly arrested. Mugabe would spend the next eleven years of his life in prison. These difficult years only strengthened his resolve to overthrow the white regime.

SOURCES—CHAPTER 1

[1] David Smith and Colin Simpson, *Mugabe* (London, Sphere Books, 1981), p. 27.
[2] The name and political status of Rhodesia has changed several times over the years. From 1889 to 1890 the country was known simply as Rhodesia. The name Southern Rhodesia was adopted in 1895. In 1923 the white settlers made Southern Rhodesia a self-governing colony of Great Britain. In 1953 Southern Rhodesia joined Northern Rhodesia (present-day Zambia) and Nyasaland (now Malawi) in a federation that lasted ten years. In 1970 the white government declared the country a republic called Rhodesia. Eight years later the nation gained a new name: Zimbabwe-Rhodesia. In 1980 the country became known as Zimbabwe.
[3] Ibid. p. 15.
[4] Ibid. p. 37.

CHAPTER 2

THE STRUGGLE FOR FREEDOM

In November 1965 the new prime minister, Ian Smith, declared Rhodesia an independent nation. Since the British had never agreed to grant independence, they refused to recognize Rhodesia as a new country. The United Nations condemned the act and called on its members to stop trading with Rhodesia. In spite of worldwide opposition, Prime Minister Smith and the majority of whites who supported him decided the time had come to chart their own, independent course.

Mugabe heard about the declaration of independence from prison, where he was living under very harsh conditions. Crowded together inside a tiny cell, Mugabe and his companions had only a bucket for a toilet and were forced to survive on meager rations.

Ian Smith became prime minister of Southern Rhodesia in 1964 on the promise of maintaining white minority rule.

Some of the prisoners died from malnutrition, others were stricken by fatal disease. But Mugabe was more fortunate. He adjusted to the rigors of prison life and survived.

Inside the prison walls Mugabe organized a school, and during the day, ZANU members attended classes to improve their education. In addition to teaching, Mugabe was also taking correspondence courses at night to earn a law degree from the University of London.

In letters smuggled through the prison gates, Mugabe and his colleagues were able to keep in touch with the ZANU leaders who remained on the outside. One of these was Herbert Chitepo, who directed guerrilla operations against Rhodesia from bases inside Zambia, a country friendly to the cause of black liberation. In April 1966 a small guerrilla band attacked and killed a white farmer and his wife. But a short time later seven of the guerrillas were slain in a 12-hour gun battle with Rhodesian armed forces. Today Zimbabwe marks the battle—April 28, 1966—as Chimurenga Day. *Chimurenga* is a Shona word that means "struggle" or "revolution," and dates to the black uprising against the white settlers in the 1890s.

These early attacks were generally unsuccessful because the guerrillas were poorly equipped and even more poorly trained. Black leaders seemed to believe that a small show of force would be enough to gain support among the vast majority of Africans inside Rhodesia. But most Africans did not flock to the guerrilla's side. They were intimidated by the Rhodesian government and fearful of the highly trained Rhodesian army. Most of the army was made up of black Africans who seemed more than willing to fight the black guerrillas. This may seem odd, but the Rhodesian army provided steady employment for many blacks who needed jobs. During the early days of the war the undisciplined guerrilla bands proved no match for the Rhodesian army, which easily defeated them in battle.

Black leaders, including Mugabe, began to realize that they were in for a long struggle. If they ever hoped to win, the guerrilla forces would have to be much better trained. Gradually, a more rigorous and more effective training program was introduced. For a new recruit, the typical day began at 4:30 in the morning with exercise and a 16-mile run. This was followed by political education: courses in the history of Rhodesia and the government's discrimination against blacks, as well as instruction in the writings of Karl Marx and Mao Zedong, the Chinese Communist leader.

From Mao the black nationalists learned about the principles of successful guerrilla warfare. First, mobilize the people in the countryside and win them over to your side. Engage the enemy only in small, hit-and-run battles. Establish bases among the people and start to attack the enemy with greater force. Finally, mount relentless assaults against the large urban centers. To reinforce these principles, Chinese instructors came to newly established guerrilla camps in Tanzania to train recruits in reconnaissance, sabotage, and other tactics.

The guerrillas' new strategy and training began to take effect in the early 1970s. Rebels moved into northeastern Rhodesia from training camps inside surrounding African countries. Most of this activity was carried out by ZANU forces under the direction of men like Chitepo. They lived among the African people, learned about their grievances against the white government, and tried to help them. From their positions inside friendly villages, the guerrillas then began to launch attacks on the white settlers.

In 1972 they struck a white family at Altena Farm in northeast Rhodesia. When battle-hardened Rhodesian forces hurried into the area, the black rebels simply melted away into the bush to avoid a pitched battle. Meanwhile ZAPU—Nkomo's organization—was also engaged in guerrilla activities inside Rhodesia. In 1973, for example, ZAPU struck a Rhodesian military camp, killing and wounding some government soldiers.

With successful hit-and-run tactics, the guerrillas were able to increase their support among the villages. One of ZANU's most important supporters, for example, was an influential spirit medium named Mbuya Nehanda. She was a very old woman who dressed in a black cloth and wore bangles around her neck and on her wrists. Among many Africans the spirit mediums hold a place of great honor, for it is through these mediums that individuals believe they can communicate with the spirits of their dead ances-

In a "protected" village, a guard checks the identity cards of all Africans returning to the village. During the guerrilla war, the white government of Southern Rhodesia hoped to discourage blacks from smuggling weapons for the nationalist forces.

tors. Mbuya Nehanda was highly esteemed by other mediums and many rural Africans living in northeast Rhodesia. Once she began working with ZANU, they followed her example and lent their support to the rebels, too.

The ZANU forces also enlisted the aid of tribal chiefs and village elders, who were the leaders and opinion-makers of the rural black communities. The rebels persuaded these men to help them hide supplies of arms that could later be used by guerrilla bands operating inside the country.

In assisting the rebels, however, the African people were taking grave risks. The white Rhodesian government placed heavy fines on villages suspected of helping the guerrillas. Villagers could lose their cattle or any of their other possessions, and even undergo brutal torture at the hands of Rhodesian security forces. Entire villages were resettled and surrounded by fences to prevent them from aiding guerrillas operating in the northeastern part of the country. And large rewards were offered to any individuals who were willing to help the Rhodesian government with information about the rebels.

During the early 1970s these tactics helped the Rhodesian forces retain control of the countryside. Although the rebels had gained some support among the villagers, many others were afraid to oppose the Rhodesian government. Guerrilla arms supplies that came from China and the Soviet Union also proved to be inadequate. They were simply no match for the helicopters and fighter planes that the Rhodesians could put into the field. Still, rebel forces continued to grow and carry on the struggle.

LIFE IN PRISON

As battles were being fought in the countryside, inside prison Mugabe was forced to deal with a different set of problems. One of these was a personal tragedy. His young son had died in Ghana, where Sally had returned to live and await her husband's release. When Mugabe received the news of his son's death, he asked the government to let him out of prison long enough to attend the funeral services. But the government refused.

While in prison Mugabe also suffered the loss of his friend and colleague, Leopold Takuwera, who died after a lengthy illness. His life might have been saved if the authorities had given him proper medical attention. Meanwhile prison life seemed to be taking its toll on another ZANU leader, Ndabaningi Sithole. For a number of months Sithole had been acting strangely, and eventually he separated himself from the other ZANU party members. He also became involved in a bizarre plot to assassinate Prime Minister Ian Smith. When the plot was discovered, Sithole was forced to stand trial for his role in it. After being found guilty, he announced: "I wish to publicly disassociate myself from... any terrorist activities and from any form of violence."

The other ZANU leaders in prison, including Mugabe, decided that Sithole was no longer fit to lead them. So they eventually forced him out and agreed that Mugabe should replace him. While some have criticized Mugabe and called him an opportunist for taking power from Sithole, many others believe that he was the most logical choice to become the new leader of ZANU.

MUGABE IS RELEASED

Every nation is affected by events occurring outside its borders. Now events began to take place outside Rhodesia that would not only influence the guerrilla war, but would also lead directly to Mugabe's release from prison.

Since Rhodesia's declaration of independence in 1965, one of its strongest allies had been South Africa, which was also run by a white minority regime. The whites in South Africa felt a close kinship with their white neighbors in Rhodesia because both were battling to preserve their way of life against the rising tide of black nationalism. South Africa had been assisting the Rhodesian government in fighting the rebels, and continued to trade with Rhodesia after most other countries throughout the world refused. South African business firms had even opened offices in Rhodesia and invested heavily in Rhodesian industries.

To the east, Rhodesia had another strong ally in the Portuguese colony of Mozambique, which stretches along the African coast. Since Rhodesia was landlocked, it depended on Mozambique's ports to provide outlets for Rhodesian products. Into Mozambique also came huge tankers carrying oil, which Rhodesia used to fuel its industries, automobiles, and military vehicles and planes.

However, the political situation in Mozambique was growing

very unstable. For years the Portuguese had been fighting black liberation forces that were trying to seize control of the country. This war, along with similar conflicts in Portugal's other African colonies, had cost the country dearly in money and lives. Suddenly, in 1974, a coup occurred that brought a new government to power in Portugal. Shortly afterward its leaders announced that the Portuguese would begin to withdraw from their colonies and grant them independence.

This meant that Rhodesia would now face, on its eastern border, a black government that might cut off all trade relations. In addition, ZANU had been receiving aid from Mozambique's black liberation forces. White Rhodesians feared that this support might increase once nationalists were in power in Mozambique.

In South Africa the government of Prime Minister John Vorster watched the events inside Mozambique with growing alarm. Vorster recognized that white Rhodesia would now be almost surrounded by black African states and could not survive much longer. Vorster also realized that if he continued to support the Smith regime, South Africa would eventually find itself alone facing a group of hostile African states that might try to undermine its government. So Vorster began to put pressure on Smith to negotiate with the black liberation leaders inside Rhodesia.

At the same time Zambian president Kenneth Kaunda hoped to persuade ZANU and ZAPU to negotiate with Smith. Kaunda wanted to end the conflict in Rhodesia as soon as possible because it was damaging the Zambian economy. Rhodesia had always been one of Zambia's primary trading partners. But following Rhodesia's declaration of independence, Zambia had cut off trade in order to show that it stood firmly against the white regime. Now Kaunda was paying a heavy price.

There's an old saying that "politics makes strange partners." That is, people who are usually enemies may occasionally decide to work together if they want the same thing. This is exactly what happened with Vorster and Kaunda. These men were political foes.

One headed a white minority government, while the other headed a black majority regime. But both of them wanted the same thing—an end to the war in Zimbabwe. Eventually, the South African and Zambian governments began meeting secretly to figure out a way to start negotiations between Smith and the guerrilla forces.

After much work some progress was achieved. South Africa pressured Smith into releasing the black liberation leaders from his jails. Mugabe and his ZANU colleagues were set free in 1974, along with Nkomo, who had also been imprisoned by the Rhodesian government. Kaunda then hoped to bring the different factions of the black liberation movement together and force them to negotiate with Smith for a gradual transition to majority rule over the next few years.

But Kaunda's efforts failed. Mugabe could not overcome his mistrust of Nkomo and his dislike for him. Nor would he accept anything less than immediate black rule. Smith had no intention of granting this demand. In fact, he never intended to give any power to the blacks as long as he remained prime minister.

Instead, Smith decided to continue the war against the guerrillas, believing that somehow he could eventually win it. This proved to be a tragic mistake.

CHAPTER 3

A NEW NATION AND A NEW LEADER

As soon as he was released from prison, Mugabe had to deal with a number of serious problems affecting not only his future but the future of ZANU. During the early part of the war, many of ZANU's leaders as well as hundreds of its soldiers were killed, and new recruits were slow to join the movement. So Mugabe immediately began a recruiting drive, with the help of two of his closest associates, Edgar Tekere and Enos Nkola. The three men crisscrossed large areas of Zimbabwe, speaking to small groups of people and urging them to join ZANU. Many in the audience listened, and they left their homes to train in the ZANU camps located in the frontline states of Tanzania and Mozambique. (The frontline states are those countries surrounding or near South

Africa. In addition to Tanzania and Mozambique, these states include Angola, Botswana, Zambia, and, in 1980, Zimbabwe.)

Mugabe did not remain inside Rhodesia long, however, for he feared that the Smith regime might decide to re-arrest all of ZANU's leaders. With the help of an old chief named Tangwena, who was not afraid of the government, Mugabe in 1974 slipped secretly across the eastern highlands and over the border into Mozambique.

Here Mugabe faced another problem. Samora Machel, the president of Mozambique, did not readily accept Mugabe as the new leader of ZANU. Like Nyerere of Tanzania and Kaunda of Zambia, Machel hardly knew Mugabe and wasn't sure he could be trusted to run ZANU. All three of the frontline leaders believed that Sithole was still the man to lead the party. As a result Mugabe and his wife, Sally, were kept under close surveillance by Machel's police during the early months in Mozambique.

Meanwhile, Mugabe was having difficulty gaining support among the battle-hardened veterans of ZANU. Many of them felt that he lacked experience as a military commander and they were, at first, reluctant to follow him. But in the coming months Mugabe would convince the guerrillas and the frontline leaders that he was the only man who could run ZANU successfully.

First Mugabe began visiting the training camps in the hills of Tanzania, where new recruits were now pouring in at a more rapid rate. Here he was able to observe the guerrilla training firsthand and talk with many of the leaders who were conducting operations in the field. From Tanzania Mugabe flew to Zurich, Switzerland, hoping to raise the money that ZANU desperately needed to continue the struggle. The beautiful old buildings of Zurich, one of Europe's wealthiest cities, must have presented quite a contrast to ZANU's impoverished tent camps in Tanzania. Mugabe did not stay too long in Zurich and only succeeded in raising a small amount of money, but he did achieve some recognition for himself as the new leader of ZANU. When Mugabe returned to Africa, the movement was clearly growing stronger and he could confidently write to all the guerrilla troops at the end of 1975: "Dear Comrades. Congratulations! ZANU is once again in full revolutionary stride."[1]

In 1976 the war widened as more guerrillas crossed into Rhodesia, destroying bridges, mining roads, attacking farms, and blowing up mills and water pumping stations. The government called up additional troops to deal with the situation, but they couldn't prevent the rebels from terrorizing the white farmers and miners. Hundreds abandoned their farms and mines, thus disrupting the Rhodesian economy. Meanwhile Samora Machel decided to close the Mozambique border with Rhodesia, cutting off trade routes and shutting down the flow of oil from the coast.

Suddenly Rhodesia found itself more than ever dependent on South Africa for economic survival, but Prime Minister Vorster was growing impatient with Ian Smith and wanted him to end the war. Britain was also pressing for a settlement, and the United States even sent its top negotiator, Secretary of State Henry Kissinger, to Africa to try to achieve peace. Smith said he was now prepared to end the fighting and permit majority rule within two years. In the meantime, he added, the whites would retain control of the government.

This was far less than frontline leaders Kaunda, Nyerere, and Machel wanted from Smith. Nevertheless, they were growing tired of the war and wished to see negotiations begin between Smith and the black nationalist force. Before the negotiations opened, however, the frontline leaders urged Mugabe and Nkomo to join their organizations together to present a strong, united front. Mugabe was reluctant to do this. He knew that Nkomo had been negotiating with Smith on his own over the past year and didn't trust the ZAPU leader. Mugabe also had no interest in negotiations; he wanted to win the war. But he could win only if he could continue operating

Geneva, Switzerland, 1976. Robert Mugabe, center, took part in negotiations to end the fighting in Southern Rhodesia. Mugabe and Joshua Nkomo, the other black nationalist leader, were too far apart in their views and the meeting broke down.

from his base inside the frontline states. Therefore, when one of the frontline leaders, Julius Nyerere, put pressure on him to join with Nkomo, Mugabe felt he had to agree. Together, in 1976, the two men formed a new political organization, the Patriotic Front (PF).

In the fall of 1976 the Patriotic Front leaders traveled to Geneva, Switzerland, to negotiate peace. The city, which lies along the shores of beautiful Lake Geneva, has long been a center for international organizations and a favorite site for peace conferences. But for Mugabe the trip to Geneva was a waste of time because he never had much intention of negotiating. As he told his soldiers before leaving Rhodesia: "What is required is the total destruction of Smith's army and immediate replacement by ZANU forces."

At Geneva Mugabe presented himself as a Marxist radical in contrast to the more moderate Nkomo. He stubbornly refused to compromise and made it clear at press conferences that there would be no place for whites in Rhodesia once the blacks came to power: "What I am saying is that we are socialists and we shall draw on the socialist systems of Mozambique and Tanzania. One cannot get rid of all the trappings of free enterprise. But in Zimbabwe none of the white exploiters will be allowed to keep an acre of their land."

The Geneva meeting, itself, achieved nothing because the two sides were simply too far apart. And the PF leaders returned home to continue the war.

ON TO VICTORY

In Rhodesia the tide of war was now clearly running against the government. The guerrillas were gaining control of the countryside, winning over the people and killing Rhodesian soldiers in numerous hit-and-run attacks. The level of terrorism and the number of atrocities on both sides increased. In February 1977 seven missionaries were murdered at St. Paul's Mission, only 25 miles from Salisbury. What looked like the work of guerrillas actually turned out to be an attack by Rhodesian security forces who were disguised as rebel troops.

In August black guerrillas set off a bomb in a Salisbury store, killing eleven people and wounding seventy-six more. Fearful of the increasing violence, each month over 1,000 white Rhodesians were packing up and leaving the country to escape the conflict.

Since the Smith regime seemed unable to destroy the guerrillas inside the country, attacks were launched at rebel camps across the border in Mozambique. Mugabe claimed these were mainly refugee camps for blacks who had fled the war, but the government contended they were primarily training areas for guerrillas. An attack in 1976 had taken the lives of almost 1,000 people, most of them refugees. And in 1977 the Rhodesians struck another camp, this time with bombers, fighter planes, and paratroopers, killing hundreds of men, women, and children.

In the meantime Smith was also hoping to defeat the rebels by dividing the black leaders who opposed his government. So far he had been unable to work out any agreement with Nkomo. But Smith did succeed in reaching a settlement with black moderates led by Methodist Bishop Abel Muzorewa and Ndabaningi Sithole (the former head of ZANU). In 1978 Muzorewa was elected prime minister of the recently renamed country of Zimbabwe-Rhodesia. Under the terms of the agreement worked out between Smith and Muzorewa, blacks and whites would now share power. Nevertheless, real control of the government still remained in the hands of Smith and his white colleagues.

Smith was gambling that this compromise would be enough to satisfy the majority of blacks. He hoped that Muzorewa and Sithole could persuade many of the guerrillas to lay down their arms, support the new government, and end the war. Once this occurred, Smith believed, the other nations of the world might lift the economic sanctions that were threatening the Rhodesian economy.

But Smith's plan failed. The new regime was immediately condemned by the Patriotic Front, and the economic sanctions were not lifted. The guerrillas also remained in the field. During 1978, 13,000 ZANU troops were already operating inside Rhodesia together with a smaller number of ZAPU forces. Mugabe called this the "Year of the People," as ZANU gradually increased its control of the rural areas and tried to cut off Salisbury from the rest of the country.

In June 1978 a particularly savage guerrilla attack occurred at Elim Mission, near the Mozambique border, in which eight missionaries and four children were murdered. Mugabe claimed that this massacre was carried out by Rhodesian army troops once again dressed up to look like rebels, but this time it seemed clearly to be the work of ZANU. However, a few months later the Rhodesian army did launch a strike—this time against a guerrilla camp in Zambia.

For Smith's brutal conduct of the war, Mugabe felt there was only one punishment—death!

> Mr. Smith is a criminal; he has committed all kinds of very serious crimes. The massacres he has committed here upon Zimbabwean refugees in Mozambique, in Zambia... warrant very stern judgment by the people. They call for the death penalty in my opinion, but again I am not the person to pronounce it... we will have him tried by the people—if by the time we take over he will still be around.[2]

NEGOTIATIONS BRING A SETTLEMENT

By 1979, its fifteenth year of independence, Rhodesia found itself struggling for survival. Thousands of whites had already fled the country. And those who remained had to cope daily with the cruelties of a war that was taking the lives of friends and neighbors and wearing down the fragile economy.

Across Rhodesia's borders the frontline states faced similar problems. Zambia's economy was already in terrible condition, while the cost of helping the rebels had become a tremendous strain for Tanzania. Meanwhile in Mozambique Samora Machel feared that continued Rhodesian raids inside his country could undermine the government.

Both Rhodesia and the frontline states needed peace, and Britain, too, was looking for a peaceful settlement to the conflict. In 1979 the British Commonwealth nations met in Lusaka, Zambia. (The Commonwealth is an organization that includes Great Britain and its former colonies.) At the Commonwealth meeting British Prime Minister Margaret Thatcher made it clear that Britain would not accept the Smith-Muzorewa government, which kept the whites in power. Instead, Thatcher called for black majority rule in Rhodesia, but with the political rights of whites carefully safeguarded. Elections would be held under British supervision to achieve majority rule, then the nation would be granted independence.

At long last it seemed as if there was a sound basis for reopening negotiations to end the war. Kenneth Kaunda and Julius Nyerere, who attended the Commonwealth meeting, both supported Thatcher's proposal. But how would the Patriotic Front react? And did Kaunda and Nyerere have enough influence on Nkomo and Mugabe to persuade them to negotiate?

Apparently they did. In September 1979 negotiations began in London at Lancaster House, an old Victorian mansion where the British had negotiated the independence of many of their former colonies. The conference, which was held under the direction of British Foreign Secretary Lord Carrington, included Robert Mugabe, Joshua Nkomo, Ian Smith, and Bishop Abel Muzorewa. Although Mugabe had agreed to attend the discussions, he really didn't believe an agreement was possible. Nevertheless, he at least seemed willing to listen.

The talks at Lancaster House continued throughout the fall, with tough bargaining on both sides. Throughout the negotiations, the frontline states kept the pressure on Mugabe to continue talking even when the discussions seemed to be breaking down. Finally, all the leaders involved succeeded in hammering out an agreement.

Under the new Zimbabwean constitution accepted at Lancaster House, blacks received 80 seats in parliament, with 20 seats reserved for whites. This guaranteed black majority rule. However, on another very important issue—the land question—black leaders had been forced to compromise. During the war Mugabe had promised that when a black government came to power, it would simply take all the land owned by whites and redistribute it to black farmers. At Lancaster House he agreed that the whites should be paid for their land. This would prove to be extremely costly for the new government and slow down any land redistribution program.

The agreements reached at Lancaster House also called on the

Peace was finally achieved in 1979 at the Lancaster House Conference in London. Robert Mugabe, far right, was one of the signers of the agreement that gave blacks control of the government.

guerrillas to come in from the bush and gather at various assembly areas throughout the country. Rhodesian security forces were expected to assemble at specific bases, too. This would prevent the war from continuing and would keep either side from trying to intimidate voters who would be participating in the upcoming elections. These elections were to be held in February 1980 to select a new government. In the meantime a British governor would run Rhodesia with the assistance of an armed force provided by the Commonwealth. After the elections the country would become independent.

AN ELECTION VICTORY

The election campaign for the 80 black seats in parliament got under way almost immediately. Nkomo wanted to run with Mugabe on a PF ticket, because he was certain that together they would win. Of course, Nkomo expected to lead the ticket himself and become prime minister. However, Mugabe simply wouldn't agree to take second place. Instead, he decided to run as head of his own party, called ZANU (PF). That left Nkomo alone to head the PF ticket against Mugabe and the third major contender, Bishop Muzorewa.

Mugabe appeared as the most radical of the three leaders, and the most to be feared by the white minority. They saw him as a "bloodthirsty Communist terrorist" who would try to transform the entire country if he were elected. But in the opening speech of his election campaign on January 27, 1980, Mugabe was conciliatory: "The State of Zimbabwe must be truly democratic... we are pledged to giving everybody, regardless of race and color, a place in society. There is, therefore, no need for anxiety or fear. We mean what we say."

Although the campaign was short, it would prove to be a stern test for Mugabe. After leaving a rally in Fort Victoria, a bomb exploded in his motorcade injuring five of his bodyguards. Mugabe immediately blamed the Rhodesian security forces for planning to assassinate him.

Meanwhile some of Mugabe's guerrilla forces had refused to leave the bush and go to the assembly areas as they were supposed to do. All along Mugabe had been afraid of bringing the ZANU guerrillas into these areas because he thought the Rhodesians might try to massacre them. In fact, clashes broke out between ZANU troops still in the field and the Rhodesian armed forces, which threatened to disrupt the elections. There were also numerous reports that ZANU guerrillas were trying to intimidate blacks into voting for the party's candidates.

When the elections were finally held on February 27–29, 1980, British police were stationed at polling places throughout the country to ensure that the voting was entirely fair and honest. The voter turnout was overwhelming; in some cases lines stretched for half a mile outside the polling booths. From the large black townships

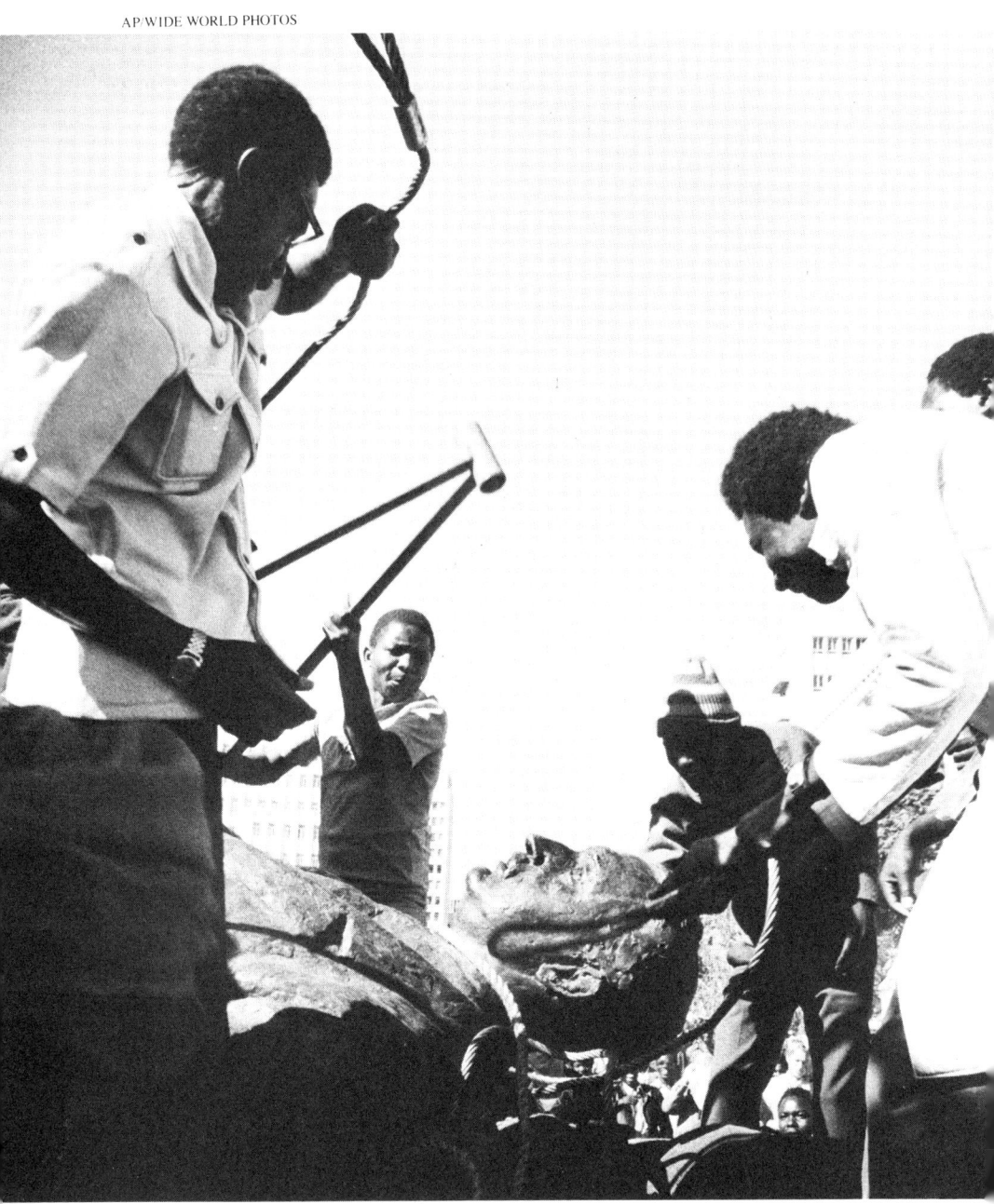

Africans celebrate the independence of Zimbabwe by flogging a statue of Cecil Rhodes, founder of Rhodesia and a symbol of colonialism.

outside of Salisbury, to the tiny villages in the bush, to the assembly areas where the guerrillas camped, blacks finally had an opportunity to vote for their own government.

And the results were decisive. ZANU (PF) won 57 seats in the new parliament, with 20 seats for the Patriotic Front and only 3 seats for Bishop Muzorewa's party. Mugabe had achieved an overwhelming victory.

Why did he win? For years ZANU had been the primary force fighting against the Rhodesian government. ZANU guerrillas had lived with the people and had organized large sections of the countryside, which voted for the party in the elections. Mugabe, as a member of the Shonas, also received wide support among the Shona people, who constituted a majority of blacks in the country. Finally, unlike Nkomo or Muzorewa, Mugabe had always refused to deal with Smith during the war. He had insisted on nothing less than immediate black majority rule, and he had achieved it.

BIRTH OF A NATION

On April 17, 1980, over 40,000 people attended an evening ceremony in Salisbury marking the birth of the fifty-first independent state in Africa—Zimbabwe. Highlighting the ceremony were parades, tribal dances, and the lighting of an eternal flame by Prime Minister Robert Mugabe to commemorate the 27,000 people who had lost their lives during the war.

Diplomats from ninety-six nations attended the festive celebration, including Prince Charles, the heir to the British throne. Addressing the people assembled that evening, Mugabe said: "Tomorrow we are born again, born again collectively as a nation of Zimbabweans. Our new mind must have a new vision and our hearts a new love and a new spirit that must unite, not divide."

Then, at one minute after midnight on April 18, the striped Zimbabwean flag was raised over Salisbury. A new era had begun.

Sources—Chapter 3

[1] David Smith and Colin Simpson, *Mugabe* (London, Sphere Books, 1981), p. 45.
[2] Ibid. p. 130.

CHAPTER 4

ZIMBABWE— A SNAPSHOT

What kind of land is Zimbabwe, the country that Robert Mugabe began to govern in 1980? Zimbabwe is a nation of ten million people. Most are black, primarily Shona and Ndebele. A small minority, approximately 200,000, are white.

The country stretches for over 150,000 square miles, making it slightly larger than Montana and somewhat smaller than California. Although it is completely landlocked, Zimbabwe's northern and southern frontiers are formed by two great rivers that empty into the Indian Ocean. In the south the broad Limpopo River forms the border with South Africa. In the north the legendary Zambezi River flows along Zimbabwe's long border with Zambia. Mozambique lies to the east and northeast, while Botswana is situated to the west.

Since Zimbabwe is located in the southern hemisphere, winter falls between May and August, while summer stretches from September until March. Summer is also the rainy season when the Zambezi swells to many times its normal size and overflows its banks. As the mighty river flows westward, it drops suddenly 350 feet into a yawning chasm to form Victoria Falls. The falls were named after Britain's Queen Victoria by the Scottish explorer and missionary David Livingstone, who first saw them in 1855 during one of his expeditions along the river. Today, if you visit Victoria Falls, you will see a statute of Livingstone standing nearby.

Eastward along the Zambezi from Victoria Falls lies Lake Kariba, the largest artificial lake south of the Sahara Desert and a popular recreation center for the people of Zimbabwe. The lake was created by the construction of the huge Kariba Dam in the 1950s. The dam generates hydroelectric power, supplying essential electricity to Zimbabwe and Zambia. The development of Kariba Dam and enormous Lake Kariba threatened the lives of vast numbers of wild animals that lived on dry land bordering the Zambezi River. In 1959 a giant rescue effort called Operation Noah saw scores of workers pitching in to save many of these animals. Among them were elephants, leopards, antelope, and rhinoceroses, which can be seen today roaming the shores and inlets of Lake Kariba.

THE VELD

A large part of Zimbabwe lies on an open, grassy central plateau 3,000 to 5,000 feet above sea level. In South Africa and Zimbabwe such plateaus are known as the high veld. The veld is generally flat except for small hills. The high elevation of the veld helps provide a temperate climate for Zimbabwe. Days are warm and evenings are cool. Winters can be chilly with frost. The climate and landscape of the veld are well suited for cattle ranching. Farming is important too, and Zimbabweans produce abundant harvests of wheat and

The Kariba Dam on the Zambezi River began operation in 1960. The dam provides hydroelectric power for Zimbabwe and its neighbor, Zambia.

maize (white corn). But these crops depend on a plentiful supply of rain during the summer months; without it the land suffers from severe drought. The veld also serves as an enormous resource for the Zimbabwean economy, containing rich deposits of minerals such as gold, platinum, and chromite.

CITIES

In the northern part of the veld lies Zimbabwe's capital, formerly known as Salisbury but renamed Harare after independence. With a population of over 700,000, Harare is Zimbabwe's largest city and a center for trade, manufacturing, and transportation.

MARGARET A. NOVICKI

Harare is the capital and largest city of Zimbabwe. The high elevation of the city helps give it a pleasant climate.

Harare is called the city of flowering trees, because purple jacaranda, red poinciana, and pink bauhinia line the broad streets and fill the city's spacious parks. Harare is a modern capital of towering hotels and large shopping malls, pizza parlors and ice cream shops, restaurants and nightclubs. It is also the site of the National Archives, with records tracing Zimbabwe's entire history, as well as the National Art Gallery and a large university. Just outside the city is a modern international airport as well as the Borrowdale Race Course, a favorite spot for Zimbabweans who enjoy horse racing. Soccer, however, is probably the most popular sport in Zimbabwe, and thousands of people crowd into huge stadiums in Harare to watch a match and cheer for their favorite team. Another popular pastime is visiting one of the wild game reserves located on the outskirts of Harare. Here visitors may observe many varities of protected animals and birds.

Unlike many countries in black Africa, Zimbabwe has a well-developed network of roads and rail lines that link its cities and towns. One of the primary links connects Harare with Bulawayo in the south, the nation's second largest city, with over 400,000 people. While Harare lies in Mashonaland (the land of the Shonas) Bulawayo is located in Matebeleland (the land of the Ndebele). In the 1800s when it was still a village, Bulawayo was the home of Lobengula, chief of the Ndebele. After his defeat the British settlers constructed a new town with broad streets laid out in a huge grid pattern. Since then Bulawayo has grown into Zimbabwe's railroad hub and a center for ranching and mining. Like Harare, the city of Bulawayo boasts lovely parks and modern office buildings, colleges, and hotels. A prime tourist attraction is the National Museum, which contains wildlife exhibits, artifacts from Zimbabwe's ancient civilization, as well as Cecil Rhodes's will and his death mask.

The burial place of Rhodes is located south of Bulawayo in the Matopos Hills, also the final resting place of many African chiefs. The Matopos Hills form a harsh yet spectacular landscape of tall rock formations and jagged cliffs on which large boulders balance precariously. Zimbabweans believe that the spirits of their long-dead chiefs live in these hills and roam the rocky pathways. Matopos is also the site of numerous caves with wall paintings thought to be the work of people who inhabited the region over two thousand years ago.

East of the Matapos Hills lies Masvingo (formerly called Fort Victoria) near the ruins of Great Zimbabwe. Masvingo, the oldest community in Zimbabwe, is another important center for mining and farming. Here huge sugar cane fields and citrus groves spread out for miles. Both are irrigated by waters from nearby Lake Kyle.

Farther east in the highlands that border Mozambique is the small city of Mutare. The area around the city contains many coffee, tobacco, and tea plantations. Tea is the national drink of Zimbabwe, while tobacco and coffee are two of the nation's primary exports.

In the east rise the Vamba and Inyangi mountains, noted for their beautiful streams and waterfalls. Located here is Mount Inyangani, the highest point in Zimbabwe, at 8,514 feet.

CITY AND COUNTRY

Many Zimbabweans live in the country's cities and their surrounding suburbs. In the suburbs outside Harare, for example, middle-class whites live much the same way they did before the nation of Zimbabwe was established. They still have well-paying jobs, they still employ servants, and they still live in comfortable homes that look out over neatly manicured lawns, beautiful gardens, and quiet swimming pools.

Although discrimination ended in 1980, few blacks can afford to move into the mainly white suburbs. Most still live in the less affluent black suburbs or in shanty towns that have sprung up around the city.

Beyond the cities lie the country's farms, ranches, and plantations. These are often huge estates owned by a small number of whites, just as they were before independence. The estates are communities unto themselves, employing a large number of black workers who live with their families in villages that have been built on the property. Since it's often too far for children to travel to school, classes are usually held on the estates. Besides doing their school work, children are also expected to plough the fields and tend the farm animals.

The day begins early on the estates, usually before sunrise. By the time the tropical sun is high over the horizon, whites and blacks—who often work side by side—have been busy for hours with all the tasks that make a plantation run, whether it grows coffee or tea, cotton or tobacco. As the day ends, white families often get together to watch the sunset at gatherings called "sundowners," while blacks gather around the fires in their villages.

THE BUSH

The vast majority of blacks in Zimbabwe live neither on the large estates nor in the cities but in the bush country. The bush presents a landscape at once simple and beautiful, yet harsh and unforgiving. The people who live there are subject to all the whims of nature—floods and drought, high winds that sweep across the plain, and epidemics that can wipe out entire families. Little wonder, then, that Zimbabweans look to their gods to help defend them from all those misfortunes. They pray to the gods for rain, for bountiful harvests, for good hunting, and for a long and prosperous life.

These traditional spiritual beliefs exist side by side with Christianity, which came late to Zimbabwe, primarily in the nineteenth century. Although the country is 60 percent Christian, many Zimbabweans look to the old gods for help in time of crisis. Zimbabweans also believe fervently that the spirits of their dead ancestors still roam the earth and can influence events. If the spirits are treated well, they can provide protection from harm. But if the spirits are neglected, they can bring down their wrath on a village. Crops will die, cattle will perish, or huts will be trampled by elephants. To ward off the evil spirits, Zimbabweans regularly consult spirit mediums to communicate with the dead and interpret their wishes. They also hold elaborate ceremonies to honor the dead and seek their favor.

Throughout the bush, spiritual life is centered in the hundreds of tiny villages spread across the Zimbabwean landscape. In each of these villages all the families belong to the same clan or ethnic group, which is ruled by a chief. Most of the homes are mud huts with thatched roofs made out of grass. However, a few well-to-do villagers may have houses built of brick or cement with roofs of corrugated iron.

MARGARET A. NOVICKI

Most Zimbabweans live in rural villages like this one. Traditional housing combines sun-dried bricks and thatched roofs.

Since villages generally have no electricity or running water, Zimbabwean families are heavily dependent on the natural environment. The day begins at sunrise, or even earlier, and work continues until the sun sets. Children are sent out to gather fire wood for cooking and lighting homes. At a nearby stream women may be heard singing or talking to their daughters as they do the washing together. Women are the main farmers. They tend the village gardens and farm small plots of land that grow maize. By grinding the maize into flour, they can bake cakes called mealies, which serve as a basic food in the Zimbabwean diet. Some women also make clothing and crafts, which they sell in the village markets.

The men of the village have different responsibilities, which include hunting game and herding their cattle or goats. Fathers expect their sons to do some of the herding, just as Robert Mugabe did when he was a boy growing up in Kutama. Fathers also teach their sons how to fish with long reeds cut from the river's edge and what kind of bait will attract the fish. Some fish like worms, but others must be lured with locusts or maggots.

Education also takes the form of lore, which is passed down to children from their parents and grandparents. The elders tell stories about great kings from long ago and the spirits of dead ancestors who still roam through the bush. Among the children's favorite stories are well-known fables about tricky hares and greedy rabbits who eventually lose everything. These stories teach the importance of sharing and helping others—values that form the foundation of village life, in which everyone must work together to survive.

Throughout Zimbabwe, village life continues much the same as it has for generations. But as the nation moves into the twenty-first century, the old ways are slowly changing.

This chapter gave you a brief overview of Zimbabwe. The following chapters provide greater detail about the country. Chapter Five examines the nation's economy. Chapter Six focuses on education and health programs, while Chapter Seven describes wildlife conservation in Zimbabwe. Chapter Eight discusses the nation's politics.

CHAPTER 5

A BLACK AND WHITE ECONOMY

Before Robert Mugabe became prime minister of Zimbabwe, he was reportedly given some advice by his close friend Samora Machel, president of Mozambique until his death in a plane crash in 1986. Like Mugabe, Machel was a Marxist who had battled for years to overthrow the white regime that ran his country. When he had finally succeeded, Machel warned the whites that he would punish them and seize their property. Frightened by this threat, all the whites left Mozambique before independence. Since the whites had run the economy and had not trained any blacks to take their place, economic conditions immediately began to decline. Mozambique has never recovered from the results of "white flight."

Samora Machel advised Mugabe not to make the same mistake that he did. So far Mugabe seems to have followed his old friend's advice. He has developed an economic policy for Zimbabwe that tries to satisfy both blacks and whites. So far his policy seems to be working.

AGRICULTURE

Zimbabwe has the most successful agriculture in black Africa. While most African countries are unable to grow enough food to feed their people adequately, Zimbabwe's farmers grow enough maize to feed the entire population. And there is often a surplus that can be exported to other African nations that need it.

In addition to maize, Zimbabwean farmers grow enough wheat to satisfy the needs of the people. The nation also produces tobacco and cotton, the main agricultural exports, as well as citrus fruits, sugarcane, and tea. Cattle ranching, although a small part of the economy, is successful, too.

Zimbabwe's agricultural program was established during the period of the white government. And under Mugabe that program has remained much the same. In the 1970s, for example, there were approximately 6,500 white-owned farms, called estates, that produced 80 percent of the crops grown in the country. After Zimbabwe became independent in 1980, some of the white farmers decided to leave rather than live under black rule. But the majority chose to remain and continue to run their estates. So far Mugabe has made no attempt to seize white-owned estates and break them up for redistribution to black farmers.

Mugabe's decision regarding the white-owned lands has disappointed many blacks. Thousands of black farmers had supported the long war of liberation in the hope of receiving some fertile land after the war was won. However, the Lancaster House agreement prevents Mugabe from taking any land unless the whites are willing to sell and the government is willing to pay for it. By the late 1980s and early 1990s the government had been able to purchase only a limited amount of land and redistribute it to about 25 percent of the nation's poor farmers. Adequate funds are simply not available to carry out a huge land redistribution program.

Other concerns have helped shape Mugabe's thinking on the subject of land redistribution. The government fears that a full-scale redistribution program might upset Zimbabwe's success in agriculture. At present the white-owned farms continue to produce the largest share of Zimbabwe's crops each year. And Mugabe seems to believe that breaking up these successful farms might reduce crop yields. Realist that he is, Mugabe knows that poor black farmers need training and equipment to help improve their productivity.

The government has taken some steps to improve the condition of black farmers. Most black Zimbabwean farmers live on communal lands, the reserves established by the white government in the nineteenth and early twentieth centuries. The soil on the communal lands is often too poor for agriculture. The government has stepped in to provide fertilizer, seeds that produce more crops, and low-interest loans to help farmers buy equipment. None of these services was ever provided by the white regime. In addition the government ensures that poor black farmers receive a fair price for their crops, which the whites had denied them. As a result of the government's efforts, black farmers in Zimbabwe now produce 40 percent of the nation's maize and cotton.

In 1988 Mugabe was awarded the African Prize for Leadership because of his efforts in achieving a "sustainable end to hunger." Upon receiving the prize, he said: "We knew we had to maintain and improve agriculture, but first of all we had to improve the style of life of the majority of the people who lived on...the communal lands."[1] Nevertheless, living conditions in these lands remain primitive. Thousands of Zimbabwean farmers try to eke out a living from the poor land as best they can. Most have a hard time just finding enough money to buy fertilizer and seeds to grow their

Zimbabwean women cleaning shelled maize kernels. These women belong to a farmer's group that has received government funds to help increase the productivity of their land.

crops. In despair, many give up farming and join the growing number of Zimbabweans who are totally landless.

Sometimes, poor farm families are able to obtain the money they need from outside sources. These sources may be young family members who find jobs in one of Zimbabwe's cities. Other youngsters may go to work in the mines or on huge estates. As welcome as the extra money may be, many parents are afraid of what may befall their children and are reluctant to see them leave the farm.

In one of his short stories, "The Setting Sun and the Rolling World," the noted Zimbabwean writer Charles Mungoshi describes what happens when a young man decides to leave his family's farm to look for work in the city. His father warns him: "Think again, you will end dead... we have a home, poor though it is, but can you think of a day you have gone without?" But the young man is determined to go. He has completed his education and wants an opportunity to use it in the city. He also resents the fact that his father wants him to stay at home. As the young man explains, "I have thought everything over, father, I am convinced this is the only way out.... The land is overworked and gives nothing now, father. And the family is almost broken up."[2]

The conflict described by Mungoshi is being played out over and over again throughout Zimbabwe. Unfortunately many young people who go to the cities are sadly disappointed with what they find there. Often there are no jobs for them. Or if they do find jobs the wages are extremely low. The low wage scale is a problem left over from the days of the white regime when blacks were paid far less than whites. Mugabe has tried to improve the situation by raising wages. But the average income for each person in Zimbabwe is still very low—only about $300 per year, about the same as in the rest of black Africa. However, as Zimbabwe's economy continues to grow, wages will probably improve.

INDUSTRY

Today Zimbabwe's industry is considered among the strongest on the African continent. A major reason is diversity.

Many African countries are heavily dependent on a single export to support their economies. In Zambia, Zimbabwe's neighbor, that product is copper. When the price of copper in the world goes up, the Zambian economy grows stronger; but when it goes down, Zambia suffers.

In Zimbabwe, the economy is not dependent on one product. The country exports agricultural products like cotton and tobacco. Zimbabwe also has a strong mining industry, with large deposits of gold, nickel, and chromite. These minerals are mined primarily in the great dike, a huge rock formation that runs along Zimbabwe's central plateau or high veld. Centuries ago the rulers of Great Zimbabwe tapped some of the area's rich gold reserves to create a flourishing empire. In addition to gold, Zimbabwe has substantial deposits of precious gemstones, including garnet, aquamarine, and the magnificent Sandawana emeralds. Mined in the Sandawana Valley, these blue-green emeralds are considered among the world's best. Finally, Zimbabwe possesses rich veins of coal located in the northern and southern lowlands. It is these enormous coal deposits that serve as a primary source of energy for Zimbabwe's manufacturing industry.

When Mugabe came to power in 1980, he inherited thriving industries that had developed under white minority rule. Since he is a Marxist, many people feared that Mugabe would direct his government to take over all the manufacturing concerns. Instead, he has left most of them alone, the same policy he has followed in dealing with the nation's huge agricultural estates. As Mugabe once explained: "We are socialist. We will espouse socialist principles, but...the country is based on free enterprise and is therefore capitalistic...and it would be a very foolish man who would immediately take over and overthrow the system."[3]

Zimbabwe manufactures the majority of products bought and sold inside the country. These include a vast array of consumer goods such as radios, televisions, cosmetics, soaps, carpets, furniture, records, shoes, and paper. The tobacco from Zimbabwe's large plantations is manufactured into cigarettes; cotton is woven into cloth and turned into clothing; cattle and pork are slaughtered for meat; and wheat and corn are processed into baked goods.

From Zimbabwe's mills come iron and steel, which are used in the manufacture of agricultural equipment for irrigation, tobacco curing, and coffee processing. With their extensive knowledge of agriculture, Zimbabweans have developed irrigation equipment and coffee-processing machines, specially suited to the local condi-

Zimbabwe's coal deposits have helped the nation to build an industrial base for manufacturing. At this mine coal is processed and loaded onto railway cars.

tions in Africa, and exported them to other nations on the continent.

Since Zimbabwe produces so many of its own products, it can limit the amount of money that must be spent on imports. Nevertheless, the nation still imports a large amount of fertilizer and manufacturing equipment from abroad. In both of these areas Zimbabwe could increase its own domestic production and reduce the bill for imported products.

A more pressing problem is minimum wages for blacks in industry, which still remain extremely low. Some blacks have been able to improve their economic situation by becoming foremen and supervisors—jobs that were not open to them under white rule. Despite these accomplishments, very few blacks have achieved the top executive levels as presidents and heads of corporations. Zimbabwe's businesses are still largely controlled by whites, a serious problem for Mugabe's government and one which still remains to be solved. As Mugabe himself has said: "Those whites we defeated are still in control. They own the mines, the factories, the commerce. They are the bosses in our own country."

PROSPECTS FOR THE FUTURE

Many world leaders consider Zimbabwe an African success story. President Mugabe has tried to satisfy the demands and concerns of both blacks and whites in order to keep the economy healthy and productive. But he still faces some serious obstacles that could affect the future health of the economy. One of these results from the country's geographical position on the African continent. Zimbabwe is landlocked and must export its goods from ports in neighboring countries. Traditionally, 80 percent of Zimbabwe's exports have passed through the ports of its southern neighbor, South Africa.

However, the relationship between Zimbabwe and South Africa's white government is not very good. Mugabe has always been an outspoken foe of apartheid, the system of racial separation and discrimination against blacks practiced in South Africa. Diplomatic relations between the two countries were cut many years ago. Mugabe has also supported the African National Congress (ANC), which has struggled for years to overthrow the white South African regime. Mugabe has even allowed the ANC—once banned inside South Africa—to establish political offices in Zimbabwe's capital, Harare.

Although his hatred of apartheid is clear, Mugabe is reluctant to cut off trade with South Africa because of Zimbabwe's dependence on South African ports. To reduce this dependence, Mugabe has been trying to develop alternate routes for his country's exports. The most direct routes lie to the east, through Mozambique to the port cities of Beira and Maputo. At present 250 miles of roadways and rail lines connect Beira to Harare. However, inside Mozambique, this trade route is under heavy attack by rebel forces trying to overthrow the government of President Chissano. Mugabe has sent thousands of troops to Mozambique to help fight the rebels and guard the route to Beira. But the cost of keeping these troops in the field is draining the government's financial resources.

Two other issues are also causing the government serious economic problems. The first is unemployment, which is approaching 20 percent. A primary cause of such high unemployment is overpopulation. Zimbabwe's economy simply cannot grow fast enough to absorb all the young people coming into the job market. The second issue is Mugabe's decision to spend heavily on health and education programs. While these programs are sorely needed in Zimbabwe, the government has been forced to go into debt to pay for them.

The next chapter will examine Zimbabwe's health and education programs, as well as its population explosion.

Sources—Chapter 5

[1]*New York Times,* Sept. 15, 1988.
[2]Charles Mungoshi, "The Setting Sun and the Rolling World,"(Boston, Beacon Press, 1989), p. 99.
[3]*Time* Magazine, March 17, 1980.

CHAPTER 6

SERVICES FOR ALL THE PEOPLE

As Zimbabwe's president, Robert Mugabe has been a champion of government programs that provide health care and education for all the people. His own experiences probably taught him how important these programs can be. Mugabe grew up in the bush where there were no doctors, nurses, or hospitals. As a boy he watched Father Jerry O'Hea battle the white Rhodesian government to get a hospital built that would treat blacks. At a time when many blacks could not even go to elementary school because of white racism, Mugabe was one of the fortunate few to receive a college diploma. For many years afterward he worked as a teacher, fully realizing that blacks must be educated if they ever wanted to run their own country. Since independence, Mugabe has made education and health care two of Zimbabwe's top priorities.

HEALTH CARE

During the days when the whites ruled Rhodesia, they took care of their own people and spent very little time worrying about the health of the blacks. Most white settlers lived in Salisbury and Bulawayo. White doctors practiced there, and modern hospitals were constructed in these cities to care for white patients. Since the races were segregated, blacks had their own hospitals in Salisbury and Bulawayo. But these were overcrowded and understaffed, with poor sanitary conditions. Many more were needed to serve the black population. In 1976 Bulawayo had only one hospital to serve 410,000 black Africans. For the 69,000 whites there were three hospitals.

Outside the cities medical facilities for blacks were even more inadequate. As one observer put it: "Three-quarters of our population are rural, yet three-quarters of our medical resources are spent in towns, where three-quarters of our doctors live."[1] Although there were some clinics in the bush, these were totally unable to provide effective health care. Instead, blacks relied mainly on tribal doctors. For centuries these doctors had used such time-tested remedies as herbal medicine and acupuncture to treat some types of disease. But thousands of blacks still died from outbreaks of measles, diphtheria, and tuberculosis. Poor medical care was one of the key reasons why blacks did not live as long as whites. In 1977 the average life expectancy for a white woman, for example, was 74. For a black woman it was 53.

Since taking office in 1980, Mugabe has succeeded in improving health care for blacks in Zimbabwe. First, he shifted the government's emphasis from the cities to the rural areas. Not only have existing clinics in the provinces been improved, over two hundred new rural health centers have been constructed. Mugabe's goal is to have one of these centers within five miles of every Zimbabwean family.

The rural health centers provide a variety of services that include delivering babies, family planning, and immunization to prevent disease. In 1982 Zimbabwe began a massive program to immunize children against diseases such as measles, tuberculosis, polio, whooping cough, and diphtheria. Since that time infant mortality has been reduced by almost 50 percent.

Immunization is only one element in the government's effort to prevent disease. Another is the primary health care program, also started in 1982. This program is staffed by village health workers—volunteers selected by their villages and then trained in Harare. These workers are similar to the so-called "barefoot doctors" of China, who were trained by the Communist regime. They treat simple medical problems in the villages, and try to promote the importance of good nutrition, immunization, and personal hygiene. To date there are over 7,000 of these health workers. Perhaps their most important achievement has been helping villages build latrines and safe wells to prevent water supplies from being polluted.

Nevertheless, poor sanitary conditions remain a severe problem in rural Zimbabwe. Many villages do not have toilets or wells. So human waste, carrying disease, often gets into a stream or pond where it pollutes the drinking water. This is a major cause of diarrhea, which claims the lives of many young children in Zimbabwe and other Third World countries. Diarrhea causes dehydration (loss of water), sapping the strength of children who are already weak from malnutrition. And in Zimbabwe an estimated one third of all children under 5 are undernourished.

The Zimbabwe Ministry of Health has called malnutrition "a national disgrace." While the country grows enough food to feed everyone, the poor still suffer because the food is unevenly distributed and they receive too little to eat. Each year an estimated 36,000 children die from malnutrition. Another 500,000 do not fully develop physically or mentally because they lack the right foods in their diets. Malnutrition may not be as severe in Zimbabwe as it is in other parts of the African continent. However, it remains a major problem left over from the days of white rule and one that Mugabe has so far failed to solve.

HOUSING

In the area of low-income housing the Mugabe government is making slow progress. With assistance from the United Nations Zimbabwe has begun to provide new homes for the poor who could not otherwise afford them. Two communities selected for the housing projects are Kwekwe and Gutu. Vaginia Churugwi, a widow, was one of the residents of Kwekwe whose life was changed by the project.

> I had been lodging in one room with my six children. The room was not only our bedroom but our kitchen and bathroom. It was terrible. My relatives did not want anything to do with us because they felt we would be a burden. Now I have my own six-room house, with electricity and a flush toilet, and my relatives do not avoid us anymore. They give us respect.[2]

While projects like those in Kwekwe and Gutu are important, they are only a beginning. Many Zimbabweans who live in the cities and the countryside still lack adequate housing, and it will take many years and huge expenditures before their living condition can be improved.

EDUCATION

Education for all Zimbabweans has been a major goal of the government since 1980. Under the white regime only 42 percent of the nation's black children attended elemenary school, and only 20 percent went on to secondary school. Many black families simply couldn't afford the cost of an education. Nor did the white minority want black children to become higly educated for fear that they

One of Robert Mugabe's goals is to make education available to all Zimbabweans. There are not enough schools for all Zimbabwe's students, so many classes have to be held in the open.

would compete for jobs or try to run the country. Instead, whites wanted a large pool of uneducated blacks who could work as cheap labor in the mines or on the estates. And they believed that blacks should only receive the education necessary to prepare them for these types of jobs.

As soon as he became prime minister, Mugabe changed the policy of discrimination in education. He announced that a primary education would be free and available to every child in Zimbabwe. Mugabe also wanted to provide children with a free secondary education, but the expense was much too high for the government to afford. Although children now attend elementary school without charge, their parents must pay for secondary school.

Even primary schooling has proven to be very expensive. Beginning in 1980 approximately three times as many children were enrolled in school as had been in the 1970s. So the government was forced to hire hundreds of new adminstrators and teachers. Finding enough qualified people was very difficult. Retired teachers were asked to come back into the classroom, foreign teachers were recruited from Australia and Great Britain, and intensive teacher-training programs were launched to train young people.

Throughout Zimbabwe parents have been encouraged to get involved at the grass-roots level to help run local schools. In many areas they have formed committees, similar to parent-teacher associations in the United States. These committees monitor the schools that are educating the children. The parents have also pitched in to build new schools or add new classrooms to old schools to handle the increasing number of students.

A CHILD'S FUTURE

Today most of Zimbabwe's children live in rural areas where they divide their days between their villages and school classrooms. If their parents own land, children are expected to help tend the goats or cattle, plant crops, and bring in the harvests. In school they take a full range of courses, including math, history, spelling, geography, and English. Although English is the official language of Zimbabwe, children are also expected to learn Shona and Ndebele. At some schools they also acquire vocational skills such as carpentry, plumbing, and electrical wiring that will help them in looking for work. However, jobs in Zimbabwe are becoming harder and harder to find. Those who expect to enter the job market with only a high school diploma are often sadly disappointed. With almost 200,000 students expected to graduate from high school each year, most will remain unemployed.

In a short story, "The Ten Shillings," Charles Mungoshi describes a young man who comes to the city with his diploma in hand and confidently expects to find work. Two years later, he is still looking: "Two years of walking up and down the city. Two years of being kicked here and there in the locations [areas set aside for blacks]. Two years of begging for food. Two years of sleeping in gutters and drainpipes. Mararapaipi, they called him...pipe sleeper."[3]

Although Mungoshi's story was published in the 1970s, the problem of unemployment still exists in Zimbabwe. The Mugabe government has responded by establishing programs to increase the number of jobs. For example, the government started a program on a farm that was abandoned by a white farmer after independence. Young men work on the farm and learn agricultural skills as they work. The farm is run as a cooperative; everyone works together and shares in the profits. The young farmers grow maize, wheat, tobacco, and nuts, which they sell on the market. While the farm provides jobs for the workers, it also pays them enough money to help support their families.

However, there are only a few of these programs in Zimbabwe. Many more are needed to help solve the unemployment problem.

The fact is that Zimbabwe's economy cannot grow fast enough to create jobs for the growing population. At present the population growth is 3.5 percent per year. This means that Zimbabwe's ten million people will double in about nineteen years. Imagine if our population doubled in that period. Where would we find homes, or schools, or jobs? Zimbabwe is already facing these problems.

In order to slow population growth, the government has initiated a family planning program that is becoming the most successful in black Africa. Its success is due to a number of factors. The program has the determined support of President Mugabe and his wife, Sally. The government has also been willing to spend enough money for family planning services that will reach a large number of people. Finally, these services have been carried out by local health workers, not by outsiders sent in from the cities. Each village selects most of the family planning staff, who are trained in Harare, to run the program. Today almost 40 percent of married women in Zimbabwe are practicing birth control, which is four times the number of those using birth control in other black African countries. As a result, the population growth has begun to decline.

Despite the success of the government's program, there is still strong opposition to family planning among many Zimbabweans. For the poor, large families often seem like a necessity. Because so many children die young, a large family ensures that some may survive. When the children grow up, they may be able to find jobs to help support their parents in old age. Children are seen as a form of social security by many poor villagers. And the poor fear their security might disappear with family planning.

Another group often opposed to family planning is Zimbabwean men, who believe that having many children is a sign of their manhood. Many women seem to agree with their husbands that they should not practice birth control. They feel their primary role is having children.

A WOMAN'S ROLE IN ZIMBABWE

Traditionally, the role of Zimbabwean women has always been to marry and bear children. Among the Shona and Ndebele, marriages were often similar to business transactions. The parents or grandparents of the bride and groom met and negotiated a bride price, or *lobola*, a sum of money to be paid by the groom's family to the family of the bride. Once these arrangements were complete, the couple could marry.

Since there was very little work available in a tribal village, a man often left after his marriage to find a job in the mines or cities. He returned home only on weekends or even less frequently to see his wife and children and bring them the money he had earned. His young wife had the backbreaking task of running the couple's farm, if they were lucky enough to have one. She planted the fields, tended the cattle, harvested the maize, and carried it to the mill to be ground into cornmeal.

Throughout Africa women commonly farm the land. Yet they frequently have no rights to the land they cultivate. For generations land in Zimbabwe was generally given to a man by his tribal chief, and it remained his property even after he married. If the couple divorced, he held on to their land and often their children. Even if her husband died, a woman often had no title to the land. Throughout Zimbabwe, women and men were simply not considered equals.

During Zimbabwe's long struggle for liberation, the role of women changed dramatically as many of them joined the guerrillas. They cooked for the soldiers in the training camps and taught the children of refugees who had fled the civil war. They carried arms and ammunition back into Zimbabwe to supply the guerrillas, served as messengers for them, and acted as their eyes and ears to alert them when government troops were approaching. Some women also trained to fight, and a few even commanded their own squads in battle. One who became famous in the liberation struggle was Teurai Ropa Nhongo, whom Robert Mugabe later appointed minister of women's affairs. She explained women's experiences in the war this way: "In the struggle we were given the same responsibilities as men. The women showed power, determination, that they were not afraid. If women were comrades and equal during the struggle, then we should be comrades and equal in reaping the fruits of that struggle."[4]

After the war was over women did not want to return to the days when they were unequal to men. They demanded a new status in Zimbabwean society, and Mugabe promised that they would receive it.

Once Mugabe became prime minister, new laws were passed increasing the rights of women. They could enter into marriage on their own without the consent of their parents and without any bride

Teurai Ropa Nhongo is Zimbabwe's minister of community development and women's affairs. She and other women who took part in the guerrilla war demanded a new role for women in society once Zimbabwe achieved independence.

price being paid. If a divorce occurred, women could retain custody of their children, and men were expected to pay child support. If a man died, his wife kept ownership of their land so she could continue farming it.

All these laws were supposed to expand women's rights. But laws alone are often not enough to change traditions deeply rooted in society. Today, for example, the majority of marriages in Zimbabwe still involve a *lobola*. Parents have been reluctant to give up the practice because it's a way for them to recover the cost of raising and educating their daughters. And women still submit to their parents' wishes because they respect and also fear them.

Although the divorce laws were changed, many men simply pay no attention to them. After a divorce they often disappear and provide no support for their families. Widows have also failed to use the law to hold on to their land after their husbands die. Sometimes they are so afraid of their husbands' families that they let them take control of the property.

This chapter has focused on the changes that President Mugabe has tried to make in Zimbabwe's social policies. While a great deal of progress has been made, some areas will take a long time to change. The government must deal with age-old tribal traditions as well as one hundred years of white racism. These obstacles are not easy to overcome.

SOURCES-CHAPTER 6

[1] Ibbo Mandaza, *Zimbabwe: The Political Economy of Transition* (London, Codestia Books, 1986), p. 368.
[2] *United Nations Chronicle,* August 1987, p. 51.
[3] Charles Mungoshi, "The Ten Shillings," *The Setting Sun and the Rolling World* (Boston, Beacon Press, 1989), p. 107.
[4] "Women in Zimbabwe," Gay Seidman, *Feminist Studies,* Fall 1984, p. 427.

CHAPTER 7

PRESERVING WILDLIFE

Zimbabwe is home to an abundance of wildlife. Across the broad savannas roam long-legged giraffes and fleet-footed antelope, large herds of zebra and wildebeests, lion prides and solitary tigers. The forests teem with baboons and monkeys and a vast assortment of tropical birds, while huge hippopotamuses lounge contentedly in the broad rivers and crocodiles slither along the banks.

When Zimbabwe was still called Southern Rhodesia, the white government established a national park system to preserve and protect the country's wildlife. Today that system stretches for 20,000 square miles, or almost 13 percent of the nation, and includes national parks, botanical gardens, game reserves, sanctuaries, and safari areas.

However, maintaining the national park system costs money, and the government is already in debt trying to pay for other services. So a program is under way to make Zimbabwe's parks and wildlife pay for themselves.

Each year some of the wildlife are deliberately killed. The Parks Department removes a portion of the animals and sells the meat and the skins to raise money for the parks. Big-game hunters are also encouraged to come to Zimbabwe and are charged a fee for safaris into the bush to kill wild animals. Hunting safaris bring in an estimated $15 million to Zimbabwe each year.

At first conservationists strongly objected to the government's wildlife policies. They argued that the government was recklessly destroying some of Zimbabwe's unique wildlife. But the government sets strict limits on the number of animals in each species that can be killed, so the overall size of their population isn't jeopardized. And by keeping their numbers at reasonable levels, the Parks Department prevents the animals from overpopulating an area and running out of food or destroying their habitat.

In addition to big-game hunters, Zimbabwe also attracts thousands of tourists, who come to see the animals in their natural surroundings and to photograph them. They may travel out to one of the large national parks like Hwange in western Zimbabwe, or to one of the smaller, privately owned game reserves. Zimbabwe law allows local farmers to set up private game reserves on their own land and to charge a fee to tourists who want to photograph wildlife or to big-game hunters who come to lead safaris. In the government's view, this is another way to preserve wildlife by making it pay for itself. It is a policy that other African countries also follow since they're too poor to bear all the costs of wildlife conservation.

THE AFRICAN ELEPHANT

One of the animals hunted in Zimbabwe is the African elephant. Zimbabwe has an abundance of them; in fact, each year 1,000 elephants must be killed to protect their habitat from overgrazing and possible mass starvation. The country encourages big-game hunters to come and shoot the elephants. Zimbabwe has also sold the ivory from elephant tusks on the world market, where it is used in jewelry and art objects. These ivory sales have earned Zimbabwe about $1 million annually.

However, in many other parts of Africa the elephant has been hunted almost to extinction. Poachers kill the animals just for the ivory and allow the carcasses to rot. With the elephant now an endangered species, countries from around the world met together at Lausanne, Switzerland, in October 1989, and voted overwhelmingly to ban the trade in ivory. One of the countries voting against the ban was Zimbabwe. The Mugabe government has decided to permit the killing of elephants to continue, and it will also continue selling ivory on world markets.

SAVING THE BLACK RHINOCEROS

While Zimbabwe allows the selected killing of many types of animals, including the elephant, one species is an exception—the black rhinoceros. In 1970 there were approximately 65,000 of these animals in Africa. Today there are fewer than 4,000. Each year thousands of animals have been slaughtered by poachers who want their horns. The horn of the black rhinoceros is highly prized as a handle for daggers. Or it may be ground up and used for medicine.

At present more than half of the remaining black rhinos are found in Zimbabwe, many of them along the Zambezi River valley. Here they have fallen prey to poachers, illegal hunters, coming across the river from Zambia. But the Zimbabwean government is trying to stop the poachers. In 1985 Mugabe authorized the country's game rangers to shoot poachers and kill them, if necessary. Some poachers have been killed, but others keep coming back and the black rhinos continue to die.

In the meantime game rangers have been trying to remove the remaining rhinos from the Zambezi Valley to safer areas. Using tranquilizer darts, they immobilize the huge animals, which weigh

Black rhinos, part of Zimbabwe's wildlife heritage.

up to 2,900 lbs. Then the rhinos are transported to game reserves in the interior of the country, which are better protected from poachers.

Other countries in Africa have also joined in the effort to protect the black rhinos. In Namibia, for example, rangers tranquilize the animals and remove their horns so they will no longer have any value to the poachers. Although wildlife officials in Zimbabwe considered this method of preserving the rhino, they rejected it. Because the black rhino uses its horn to forage for food in the bush, removing it could be as harmful as poaching.

Meanwhile, Zimbabwe has joined with the World Wildlife Fund in an attempt to stop the international trade in rhino horns. This effort is aimed at countries that turn a blind eye to poachers and allow them to bring the horns across their borders.

WILDLIFE CONSERVATION IN THE THIRD WORLD

In Third World countries conservation cannot always be given the high priority that we give it in the industrialized countries. One reason is the poverty of Third World countries. Their leaders must decide how to spend their small funds. And feeding the hungry and employing workers must come before wildlife conservation when budgets are drawn up. Traditional attitudes pose a problem, too. Many farmers regard wildlife as their enemy because wild animals often destroy crops and kill goats or cattle.

Nations like Zimbabwe are currently attempting to make wildlife conservation an important concern. The Mugabe government is trying to re-educate some of the Zimbabwean people to understand the value of wildlife. The government is also trying to devise unusual ways to finance conservation. By preserving its wildlife, Zimbabwe is safeguarding a rich treasure for *all* future generations —African and non-African alike.

CHAPTER 8

POLITICS IN ZIMBABWE

Since 1980 Robert Mugabe has achieved success in a number of different areas such as health care, education, the economy, and wildlife management. But by far his biggest challenge has been trying to bring unity to a country with a mixed population—black and white, Shona and Ndebele.

When Mugabe came to office, whites feared that he might do the same thing that Samora Machel had done in neighboring Mozambique. Mugabe was an outspoken Marxist, and ZANU (PF) was a Marxist party. In fact, all the citizens of Zimbabwe are called "comrades" and the president is known as Comrade Mugabe.

At independence, thousands of whites fled the country. Included among them were many of Zimbabwe's white civil servants who went to live in South Africa. Fortunately, ZANU had a number of well-educated blacks who could take their places. Among the party's top officials, many had attended school in the United States. Nevertheless, the whites who remained in the government looked down on these new black civil servants. Whites had been used to running the country themselves and believed that blacks would be unable to do it. They resented the higher taxes that ZANU passed to improve education and health care. White business leaders were also reluctant to let blacks move up into positions of management.

At first there was enormous tension between whites and blacks in Zimbabwe. Whenever society changes, people often feel uncertain about the future. Whites were fearful of losing what they had achieved. Blacks expected to achieve what whites had so long denied them.

Since he came to power, Mugabe has tried to walk a path between the two races. He has let whites live much as they did before 1980 because he needs their help to make Zimbabwe run effectively. At the same time, Mugabe has improved the lives of many blacks. However, a large number are still disappointed because they have no land and no jobs.

Mugabe's policy is one of compromise. It may not work, but so far it seems to have led to fairly smooth relations between whites and blacks. Recently, for example, whites praised Mugabe for his education and health programs. And some whites who left Zimbabwe in the early 1980s have now returned. Many blacks have also given strong support to Mugabe's policies—policies that have made their nation one of the few success stories on the continent of Africa.

MUGABE AND NKOMO

Mugabe has tried to achieve good relations between blacks and whites to preserve the unity of Zimbabwe. But he has seemed far less concerned about relations between the Shona and the Ndebele.

Of a population that totals 10 million Zimbabweans, about 7 million are Shona and 1 million are Ndebele. There has been enmity between the two groups since the nineteenth century, when the Shona were conquered by the fierce warriors of the Ndebele. Tribal hatred continued during Zimbabwe's war for independence. It was symbolized by the enmity between Robert Mugabe, a Shona, and Joshua Nkomo, an Ndebele.

When Mugabe became prime minister in 1980, he tried to bring some unity between Shona and Ndebele. Nkomo and a few of his colleagues in ZAPU were invited to join the cabinet, and for a time they helped govern the country. But while the two leaders sat together in cabinet meetings, their followers clashed in bloody battles. These broke out when Mugabe tried to create a new Zimbabwean army that included his own guerrillas, Nkomo's followers, and some of the white soldiers who had fought in the civil war. But the army was not large enough to accept everyone. Many of Nkomo's guerrillas—Ndebeles—were left out. They believed Mugabe was showing favoritism to his own guerrillas—mainly Shona—and they didn't like it.

Eventually, some of Nkomo's followers decided to join a group of rebels who were already operating in Matebeleland, where most Ndebele live. There they began ambushing white farmers and murdering their families, creating unrest throughout the countryside.

Meanwhile the uneasy alliance between Nkomo and Mugabe was coming apart. Robert Mugabe has never made a secret of his desire to turn Zimbabwe into a one-party state. Many other African leaders have done the same thing in their countries. They believe that a single political party brings unity to a nation made up of a number of different groups. There are serious drawbacks to one-party rule, however. One-party rule brings great power to the party leader and can lead to abuses of power. Mugabe wanted ZANU to be the only party in Zimbabwe. This threatened Nkomo and the other members of ZAPU. They feared that a single party run by the Shona might not respect the rights of the Ndeble.

From his position inside the cabinet, Nkomo began to critize the way Mugabe was running the government. He disagreed, for example, with the prime minister's efforts to take control of Zimbabwe's free press. Then, in 1982, a supply of weapons was found on land belonging to Nkomo and other ZAPU members. Mugabe accused Nkomo of plotting against the government and fired him.

"We have a cobra in our house," Mugabe said, referring to Nkomo. "The only way to deal with a snake is to cut off his head." Nkomo was outraged. "Mugabe tries to smear me," he said, "with all that I've done for this country."[1]

After Nkomo left the cabinet, more of his former guerrillas decided to join the rebels in Matebeleland. The murder of white farmers increased, tourists were kidnapped, and ZANU politicians were killed. Some of the supplies to the rebels were coming in from South Africa, whose leaders wanted to undermine the Zimbabwean government. Mugabe is a strong foe of white racism, and the South Africans have been eager to reduce his power and perhaps see him overthrown.

To deal with the situation in Matebeleland, Mugabe sent in a specially trained force called the Fifth Brigade. With their distinctive red berets, these troops would arrive at a village and begin to terrorize its inhabitants. They used the worst forms of torture to obtain information from frightened villagers about the rebels. Anyone suspected of helping them might be immediately shot without trial. During 1983 at least 1,500 villagers in Matebeleland were killed and thousands of others were tortured.

A report from the Catholic bishops of Zimbabwe called the violence in Matebeleland "a reign of terror caused by wanton killings, woundings, beatings, burnings and rapings."[2]

In another report, *Zimbabwe: The Wages of War*, the Lawyers Committee on Human Rights stated that the Mugabe government had launched a brutal campaign against the Ndebele that included torture, murder, arrests, and imprisonments for hundreds of civilians. As the report put it:

> ... the counterinsurgency tactics used by Zimbabwe's police and security forces have been all but indistinguishable from those used by the police and security forces under former Prime Minister Ian Smith during the last years of white rule. In some instances, it has been reported that the same personnel, black and white, have been deployed ... to carry out the detentions and abductions of opposition supporters.[3]

Mugabe accused Joshua Nkomo of being directly responsible for the rebel activities that led to the violence. Although Nkomo denied the accusation, he was kept under virtual house arrest for weeks at a time. One day, after he had been able to slip out of his home, it was ransacked and his driver brutally killed. Fearing for his life, Nkomo fled the country in March 1983 and went to England. "Mugabe is trying to kill me," he said.

Later that year Nkomo returned to Zimbabwe. Meanwhile the violence was continuing. Early in 1984 the government placed a 24-hour curfew on Matebeleland. The curfew meant that people could not even go to work and earn a living. And there were other hardships. The nation was suffering through a severe drought that reduced the amount of available food. The Mugabe government prevented emergency food and medicine from reaching Matebeleland, thus increasing the misery of the Ndebele.

In the meantime the rebels in Matebeleland continued their campaign of terror. At the funeral of a ZANU party member killed by the rebels, Mugabe vowed to stop them. "I shall give power to the police, the security forces, all of them," he said, "to mount a manhunt, not only in houses, but also in bushes, ant hills and trees."[4] Throughout Zimbabwe, riots and demonstrations broke out against the ZAPU party. In addition, the government ordered ZAPU to halt all its meetings.

In November, after the rebels had killed another ZANU party member, Mugabe fired the last remaining ZAPU ministers in his cabinet. "We cannot have in our cabinet representatives of an organization dedicated to a deliberate policy of violence and banditry," he said.[5]

The following year, 1985, Mugabe called for new parliamentary elections. Clearly, he hoped to increase ZANU's majority and reduce the number of seats held by ZAPU. More seats in parliament would increase his control of the country. Before the election Nkomo accused the government of trying to frighten voters into supporting ZANU. According to the Lawyers Committee on Human Rights. "At least 80 local ZAPU officials and supporters, perhaps as many as 400, were abducted from their homes by unidentified gunmen. Few have been seen or heard from since; most are presumed to be dead." In this atmosphere of fear, many Zimbabweans did support ZANU, and after the final votes were counted, the party picked up several additional seats in parliament.

However, ZAPU still held on to some of its power. The party won the parliamentary seats in Matebeleland and continued to run the local government there. So Mugabe decided to use stronger measures to bring ZAPU under his control. After the elections were over, he ordered the arrest of some of the ZAPU leaders, including five members of parliament and the mayor of Bulawayo. Amnesty International, a human rights organization, also reported that torture in Matebeleland was continuing. "Many (are) reported to be beaten with . . . rhinoceros-hide whips, rubber hoses or sticks. Some victims (were) said to be hung upside down and beaten, with their heads in buckets of water."[6]

TOWARD UNITY

The government was now using every means available against ZAPU, and Nkomo feared his party might be destroyed. So in October 1985 he decided to sit down with Mugabe and begin talks to unite their two parties. The talks would continue for more than two years, as both leaders tried to reach an agreement. It wasn't

Robert Mugabe at a political rally. A teacher, theoretician, and practical politician—Robert Mugabe has worked to bring social justice to Zimbabwe through socialism. His critics accuse him of using dictatorial methods in shaping the nation's future.

easy, because each man was a tough negotiator. And neither one liked or trusted the other.

On several occasions the talks broke down when the men disagreed over an important issue. Then Mugabe increased the pressure on Nkomo and ZAPU to resume the discussions. When the talks were broken off in April 1987, for example, Mugabe ordered the police to raid all of the ZAPU offices in Matebeleland. He also banned the party from holding any meetings. As a result Nkomo decided to re-open discussions.

Finally, in December 1987 Mugabe and Nkomo signed an

agreement uniting their two parties. "We are one," Mugabe said afterward. That December Mugabe also formed a new government. The position of prime minister was eliminated and Mugabe became president of Zimbabwe, with Nkomo as one of his vice presidents.

In an election held during 1990, Mugabe won almost 80 percent of the vote for president against only minor opposition. ZANU took 116 out of 120 seats in the Zimbabwean Parliament. As Mugabe put it, this is a "resounding victory" and " a mandate to create a one-party state."

Now that Mugabe has achieved his goal of a single-party state, what will happen in Zimbabwe? Perhaps he hoped that once Nkomo was part of the government, the Ndebele guerrillas might stop their activities in Matebeleland. However, the guerrillas are continuing to operate there.

Perhaps Mugabe also expects to increase his power. Across the entire continent of Africa, nations are ruled by a single party and a single leader. Freedom is greatly restricted. And those who dare to speak out against the government are usually thrown into jail, or killed. Mugabe claims that he does not intend to turn Zimbabwe into a police state. After becoming president, he said, "Executive power can never rightly be a one-man show." Mugabe is reportedly willing to listen to the advice of other leaders in the government. However, Zimbabwe can hardly be called a democracy. Mugabe has shown repeatedly that he is willing to use force to achieve his goals. Time and again he has violated the civil rights of the Ndebele, who were brutally terrorized, tortured, and murdered during the government's war in Matebeleland. These scars will not heal easily.

MUGABE AND ZIMBABWE

This book has presented a portrait of Zimbabwe and its president, Robert Mugabe. More than any other man, Mugabe has been responsible for the development of modern Zimbabwe.

PAUL WEINBERG/IMPACT VISUALS

These young Zimbabweans will lead their nation into the twenty-first century. What does the future hold for them and their homeland?

Like most Zimbabweans, Mugabe has his roots in the rugged bush country where he received much of his education. Mugabe used this education, first to teach other black Zimbabweans about their heritage, then to exhort them to fight against white racism, and finally to lead them in a bloody civil war against the white regime that had run Zimbabwe for almost one hundred years. When Mugabe became the leader of ZANU, many thought that the reserved and studious former school teacher would never be able to direct guerrilla forces. But he surprised them. Alone among the black nationalists—Nkomo, Muzorewa, Sithole—Mugabe refused to negotiate with the whites and fought for total victory. Many called him stubborn and egotistical. But in 1980 he proved that victory was possible.

That same year Mugabe became Zimbabwe's first prime minister in a lopsided election that surprised many people. But perhaps the biggest surprise came when Mugabe showed that he was willing to work together with whites to make the new nation of Zimbabwe prosper. Mugabe had always been the most radical of Zimbabwe's leaders—a fiery nationalist and an outspoken Marxist. Suddenly, he appeared to put aside his radical views and became a champion of capitalism as well as racial harmony between blacks and whites.

Why did Mugabe change? Or did he? Above all, Mugabe seems to be a practical politician who is looking for policies that succeed. He is willing to work with whites if it means that Zimbabwe can grow enough food to feed its people. He is also willing to preserve capitalism if it means jobs for Zimbabweans and money to pay for education and health care programs. On a continent where so many governments have failed, Mugabe is determined to make Zimbabwe succeed.

However, the nation faces some enormous problems. Zimbabwe has a rapidly growing population and rising unemployment. The majority of black farmers still live on very poor land. And many Zimbabweans are completely landless. Finally, the bitter conflict between Mugabe and Nkomo—between Shona and Ndebele—has sharply divided the nation. And Mugabe's desire for supreme authority has alienated many Zimbabweans. In the 1990 election, for example, only about 54 percent of the people voted as compared to 95 percent in past elections.

Nevertheless, Robert Mugabe stands at the peak of his political power. Now we must ask: What will he do with it? How will he deal with the problems facing Zimbabwe? Where will he lead the country? What does the future hold for Mugabe and Zimbabwe in the twenty-first century?

Sources—Chapter 8

[1] *Facts on File*, March 1982.
[2] Bishops Pastoral Statement, March 27, 1985.
[3] Lawyers Committee on Human Rights, *Zimbabwe: The Wages of War* (New York, 1986), p. 4.
[4] *Facts on File*, May 1983.
[5] *Facts on File*, Nov. 1984.
[6] Jack Shepherd, "Zimbabwe—Poised on the Brink,"*Atlantic*, July 1987.

TIME LINE

A.D. 1000	Great Zimbabwe at its height
1450	Shona kings abandon Great Zimbabwe
1652	Dutch establish Cape Colony in southern Africa
1870	Cecil Rhodes arrives in southern Africa
1886	Gold discovered in southern Africa
1890	Pioneer Column sets out from Cape Colony; Salisbury founded
1893	Defeat of Lobengula
1896–1897	Chimurenga between Africans and British ends in African defeat
1902	Death of Cecil Rhodes
1914–1918	World War I
1923	Southern Rhodesia becomes a self-governing British colony
1924	*Robert Mugabe born in Kutama*
1939	World War II begins
1943	*Robert Mugabe graduates from teacher training school*
1945	World War II ends
1955	City Youth League established
1958	*Robert Mugabe travels to Ghana*
1960	National Democratic Party (NDP) formed
1961	*Robert Mugabe marries Sally Hayfron;* ZAPU formed
1963	ZANU formed; *Robert Mugabe jailed*
1965	Ian Smith declares Rhodesia an independent country
1966	Guerrilla war breaks out in Zimbabwe
1974	*Robert Mugabe released from jail*
1976	Mugabe and Nkomo meet in Geneva to negotiate a peace settlement; talks break down
1979	Lancaster House Agreement provides for black majority government in Zimbabwe

1980	Zimbabwe achieves independence; *Robert Mugabe elected prime minister*
1982	Primary health care program started
1987	ZANU and ZAPU united; *Mugabe forms a new government with himself as president*
1988	*Mugabe awarded Africa Prize for Leadership*
1990	Zimbabwe celebrates its tenth anniversary of independence

GLOSSARY

African National Congress (ANC) The oldest and most powerful black nationalist organization in South Africa; once banned by the white South African government, the ANC has been allowed to set up political offices in Zimbabwe and Zambia.

Bulawayo (boo la WAY yo) A large city in southern Zimbabwe; the nation's second largest city.

Chikerema, James (chi kuh RAY mah) A black nationalist who helped form the City Youth League.

Chimurenga (chi moo REN gah) A Shona word meaning "struggle" or "revolution." Zimbabwe has set aside April 28, 1966—Chimurenga Day—to remember the gun battle that took place between blacks and Rhodesian armed forces on that day. Also, the name given to the black uprising against white settlers in the late 1890s.

City Youth League   Founded in 1955, the league helped to awaken black nationalism in Southern Rhodesia by calling for strikes by black workers.

communal lands   In Zimbabwe, the former reserves set aside by the white government for blacks; most poor black farmers in Zimbabwe live on communal lands.

estates   In Zimbabwe, the white-owned farms that produce a large percentage of the nation's crops.

frontline states   The countries surrounding or located near South Africa: Tanzania, Mozambique, Angola, Botswana, Zambia, and Zimbabwe. The leaders of the frontline states regard South Africa as a destructive force in the region and have been involved to varying degrees in trying to bring about black majority rule in South Africa.

game reserve   In Africa, areas set aside by the government for the protection of wildlife. Game reserves are major tourist attractions in Zimbabwe and other African nations.

Great Zimbabwe   A royal city built by the Shonas almost a thousand years ago; the site of Zimbabwe's ancient civilization.

Harare (ha RA re)   The capital of Zimbabwe; formerly called Salisbury.

Kaffir (KAF er)   A disparaging European name for Africans.

Kaunda, Kenneth (ka OON da)   The president of Zambia.

Kutama (koo TA ma)   The village where Robert Mugabe was born.

Lake Kariba (kuh RE ba)   An enormous lake formed by the huge Kariba Dam on the Zambezi River.

Lancaster House   The meeting place in London, England, where negotiations were held that ended the guerrilla war in Rhodesia and led to black majority rule in Zimbabwe.

land redistribution   In Zimbabwe and other African nations, the government's plan to take land away from European owners, divide it into small parcels, and give it to blacks.

Limpopo River (lim PO po)   A major river in southern Zimbabwe; the Limpopo forms the border between Zimbabwe and South Africa.

Lobengula (lo ben GU la)   The Ndebele chief who was defeated by the British in 1893.

lobola (lo BOW la)   A bride price; in Zimbabwe the sum of money to be paid by a groom's family to the family of the bride.

Machel, Samora (ma CHEL, sa MO ra)   The former president of Mozambique and a friend of Robert Mugabe.

maize   White corn; the chief food crop of Zimbabwe and a staple of the Zimbabwean diet.

Masvingo (mas VEEN go)   The oldest community in Zimbabwe; the ruins of Great Zimbabwe are located nearby.

Matebeleland (mat uh BE le land)   In Zimbabwe, land of the Ndebele.

Matopos Hills (ma TOE pos)   An area in southern Zimbabwe with stark landscape; the burial place of many African chiefs and also of Cecil Rhodes.

mealies   A cake made from ground maize; a basic part of the Zimbabwean diet.

Mount Inyangani (in YAN gan ee)   The highest point in Zimbabwe at 8,514 feet; located in the eastern part of the country.

Mozambique (moe zam BEEK)   A country located on the eastern coast of Africa; a neighbor of Zimbabwe's. Mozambique has several ports important to landlocked Zimbabwe.

Mugabe, Robert, (moo GA bay)   The president of Zimbabwe.

Mungoshi, Charles (mun GO shee)   A noted Zimbabwean writer; author of *The Setting Sun and the Rolling World*.

Mutare (moo TA re)   A small city in the eastern highlands of Zimbabwe; surrounded by coffee, tobacco, and tea plantations.

Muzorewa, Bishop Abel (moo za RAY wa)   The former prime minister of Zimbabwe-Rhodesia.

National Democratic Party (NDP)   A black nationalist organization started in 1960 by Michael Mawema and Leopold Takuwera. Joshua Nkomo was its first leader.

Ndebele (en da BE le)   The second largest ethnic group in Zimbabwe.

Nkomo, Joshua (en KO mo)   Vice president of Zimbabwe and leader of the Zimbabwe African People's Union (ZAPU); both colleague and foe of Robert Mugabe.

Nkrumah, Kwame (en KRU mah, kwa mee)   The first prime minister of Ghana.

Nyerere, Julius (ni RAIR ee)   The first president of Tanzania.

Patriotic Front (PF)   A political organization started by Robert Mugabe and Joshua Nkomo for the purpose of negotiating a peace settlement to the guerrilla war with white-ruled Rhodesia.

Pioneer Column   A group of white settlers and police organized by Cecil Rhodes in 1890 for the purpose of mining for gold in Matebeleland.

reserves   Barren and unproductive lands set aside for Africans by the white regime of Southern Rhodesia.

Rhodes, Cecil   The British imperialist who seized the lands of the Ndebele and Shona, turned them over to white settlers, and founded the territory that became Rhodesia.

Rhodesia (ro DEZ zhah)   The former name of Zimbabwe.

Rhodesian Front (RF) In the 1960s and 1970s, the white-supported political party in Rhodesia opposed to black nationalist demands. The RF was led by Ian Smith.

Salisbury Former name of Zimbabwe's capital when the nation was called Rhodesia; now called Harare.

Shona (SHO na) The largest ethnic group in Zimbabwe; the founders of Great Zimbabwe.

Sithole, Ndabaningi (sit O la, en da ba NIN gee) The first head of the Zimbabwe African National Union (ZANU).

Smith, Ian The leader of the Rhodesian Front party and prime minister of Rhodesia from 1964 to 1978.

spirit medium In Africa, an individual through whom the spirits of dead ancestors are belived to communicate with the living.

Takuwera, Leopold (ta ka WE ra) One of the founders of the National Democratic Party (NDP).

Tanzania (tan zan EE ah) A country located on the eastern coast of Africa.

veld (velt) A generally flat, grassy plateau found in southern Africa. A large part of Zimbabwe lies on the veld.

village health workers Volunteer health workers who bring health care to the people of rural Zimbabwe.

Zambezi (zam BE zee) A major river in northern Zimbabwe; flows along the border with Zambia.

Zambia (ZAM be ah) A nation that borders Zimbabwe on the north; formerly known as Northern Rhodesia.

Zimbabwe African National Union (ZANU) A black nationalist organization that broke off from ZAPU (Zimbabwe African People's Union) in 1963. Also a political party—ZANU (PF)—whose leader is Robert Mugabe.

Zimbabwe African People's Union (ZAPU) A black nationalist organization founded in 1961 and led by Joshua Nkomo.

BIBLIOGRAPHY

Books

Astrow, Andee. *Zimbabwe—A Revolution That Lost Its Way?* London: Zed Books, Ltd., 1983. Describes the civil war in Zimbabwe and the early years of Mugabe's leadership following independence.

Laurie, Jason. *Zimbabwe*. Chicago: Children's Press, 1988. A highly readable introduction to Zimbabwe—its geography, economy, history, and social customs.

Lawyers Committee on Human Rights. *Zimbabwe: The Wages of War*. New York, 1986. Provides a detailed account of the human rights violations during the struggle between Mugabe and Nkomo in the 1980s.

Mandaza, Ibbo (ed.). *Zimbabwe: The Political Economy of Transition, 1980–1986*. London: Codesria Books, 1986. A highly technical study of various aspects of Zimbabwe, including agriculture, industry, health care, and human rights.

Martin, David, and Johnson, Phyllis. *The Struggle for Zimbabwe*. New York: Monthly Review Press, 1981. Provides the best account of the civil war in Zimbabwe.

Mungoshi, Charles. *The Setting Sun and the Rolling World*. Boston: Beacon Press, 1989. An excellent collection of short stories that provides valuable insights into Zimbabwean society.

Smith, David, and Simpson, Colin. *Mugabe*. London: Sphere Books, 1981. The only biography of Mugabe and a highly readable account of his life up to his becoming prime minister.

Stark, Al. *Zimbabwe—A Treasure of Africa*. Minneapolis: Dillon Press, 1986. Provides a valuable description of Zimbabwe for young people.

Stoneman, Colin, and Cliffe, Lionel. *Zimbabwe: Politics, Economics and Society*. London: Pinter Publishers, 1989. Offers a detailed study of current political and economic issues in Zimbabwe.

Winchester, Gay. *Let's Visit Zimbabwe*. London: Gould Burke Publishing Co., 1982. One of the best brief surveys of Zimbabwe for young people.

Zimbabwe: A Country Study. Washington, D.C.: U.S. Government Printing Office, 1983. A dry but very valuable overview of the country.

Periodicals

"Black Power and White Fears" by Peter Webb and Holger Jensen, *Newsweek*, March 7, 1980.

"The House on Freedom Street" by Simomo Mubi, *U.N. Chronicle*, August 1987.

"Making Wildlife Pay Its Way" by Marilyn Acheron, *International Wildlife*, 1987.

"Mugabe Faces His Partner" by Joseph Treen and Holger Jensen, *Newsweek*, March 1, 1982.

"Mugabe's Win," *Time*, July 15, 1985.

"Nkomo's Bitter Homecoming" by Fay Willey, Peter Younghusband, and Tony Clifton, *Newsweek*, August 29, 1983.

"Nkomo's Dash into Exile" by John Brecher, Peter Younghusband, and Holger Jensen, *Newsweek*, March 21, 1983.

"No Instant Garden of Eden" by Rush Hoyle and Marsh Clark, *Time*, November 2, 1981.

"One Party State," *Time*, August 20, 1984.

"Overcoming Zimbabwe's Vulnerabilities" by Richard Hull, *Current Affairs*, May 1988.

"Rising Racial Tensions" by Russ Hoyle and Marsh Clark, *Time*, January 18, 1982.

"Struggle for Southern Africa" by Robert Mugabe, *Foreign Affairs*, Winter, 1987.

"Terrorists Shatter Mugabe's Peace" by Holger Jensen, *Newsweek*, August 9, 1982.

"A Troubled Success Story" by Angus Deming and Ray Wilkinson, *Newsweek*, July 15, 1985.

"Women in Zimbabwe" by Guy Seidman, *Feminist Studies*, Fall 1984.

"Zimbabwe: From Supermarket to Cafeteria" by H. Anenden, *World Health*, June 1987.

"Zimbabwe—Poised on the Brink" by Jack Shepherd, *Atlantic*, July 1987.

"Zimbabwe's Elusive Quest for Unity" by Richard Hull, *Current History*, May 1986.

"Zimbabwe Leader Tells of Food Gains" by Michael Kaufman, *New York Times*, September 18, 1988.

INDEX

Africa, 15, 93. *See also* specific countries
African elephant, 82–83
African National Congress (ANC), 21, 22, 24, 68, 99
African Prize for Leadership, 63
Agriculture, 53–54, 62–65
ANC. *See* African National Congress
Animals, 53, 56, 81–85. *See also* specific animals

Beira, 69
Birth control, 76–77
Black rhinoceros, 83–84
Blacks
 discrimination against, 18
 in Ghana, 23–24
 hospitals for, 21, 70, 71
 labor, 17, 22, 68
 in Rhodesia, 32–35, 43
 in Southern Rhodesia, 22, 24–26, 28
 in Zimbabwe, 46, 50
British Commonwealth, 45–46
Bulawayo, 17–18, 22, 27, 56, 71, 99
Bus fares, 22
Bush country, 58–60

Cape Colony, 15
Carrington, Lord, 46
Chikerema, James, 22, 99
Children, 75, 77. *See also* Education
Chimurenga Day, 32, 99

Chimurenga war, 17, 100
Chissano, President, 69
Chitepo, Herbert, 32, 33
Christianity, 20, 58
Churugwi, Vaginia, 73
Cities, 54–57, 65. *See also* specific cities
City Youth League, 22, 100
Climate, 53–54
Coal, 66, 67
Communal lands, 100
Communism, 21
Conservation, 85
Copper, 65
Cotton, 22, 62, 63, 65, 66

Diarrhea, 72
Divorce, 80
Economy, 62, 68–69
Education, 60, 69, 70, 73–75
Elephants, 82–83
Elim Mission, 44
Emeralds, 66
England. *See* Great Britain
Estates, 57, 100
Exports, 68–69

Family planning, 76–77
Farming. *See* Agriculture
Fifth Brigade, 89
Frontline states, 39–40, 100

Game reserve, 82, 100
Gandhi, Mahatma, 21
Gemstones, 66
Geneva (Switz.), 42, 43
Ghana, 23–24, 25, 26
Gold, 66
Great Britain, 15, 16, 22, 23, 26, 30, 41, 45–46
Great Zimbabwe, 13–15, 66, 100
Guerrilla warfare, 32–35, 40–41, 43–44, 78, 88, 89
Gutu, 73

Harare, 54–56, 68, 100. *See also* Salisbury

Health care, 69–72, 103
Hospitals, 21, 70, 71
Housing, 73
Hunting, 82
Hwange, 82

Immunization, 72
Imperialism, 15–16
Imports, 67
Industry, 65–67
Ivory, 13, 83

Jesuits, 19–21

Kaffir, 17, 100
Kariba Dam, 53
Kaunda, Kenneth, 37–38, 40, 41, 46, 100
Kimberley, 15
Kissinger, Henry, 41
Kutama, 19, 21, 100
Kwekwe, 73

Labor, 17, 22, 68. *See also* Unemployment
Lake Kariba, 53, 100
Lancaster House Conference, 46, 47, 100–101
Land, 46, 52, 53, 62–63, 78, 101
Lawyers Committee on Human Rights, 89, 91
Limpopo River, 15, 52, 101
Livingstone, David, 53
Lobengula, 15, 16, 17, 56, 101
Lobola, 77, 80, 101

Machel, Samora, 40, 41, 45, 61–62, 86, 101
Maize, 54, 59, 62, 63, 76, 101
Malnutrition, 72
Mandela, Nelson, 21
Mao Zedong, 33
Marriage, 77, 78, 80
Marx, Karl, 21, 33
Marxism, 86
Mashonaland, 56
Masvingo, 56, 101

Matebeleland, 15–16, 56, 88, 89, 90, 91, 92, 101
Matopos Hills, 56
Mawema, Michael, 25
Mealies, 59, 101
Medical care. *See* Health care; Hospitals
Minerals, 66
Mining, 66
Mount Inyangani, 57, 101
Mozambique, 36–37, 39–40, 41, 43, 45, 61–62, 69, 86, 101
Mugabe, Robert
  agricultural policy, 62–63
  compromise policy, 86–87
  early years, 19–21
  economic policy, 68–69
  education, 20–22, 31–32
  election, 48, 50
  in Geneva, 42–43
  imprisonment, 29–32, 35
  on independence day, 50
  industrial policy, 66
  at Lancaster House talks, 46
  and national Democratic Party, 24–26
  and Nkomo, 88–93, 95
  release from prison, 38
  and Smith, 45, 50
  social policies, 70, 71, 73, 74, 76, 78
  speech in Salisbury, 11, 13, 24–25
  teaching years, 21, 23, 24
  and Zimbabwe African National Union (ZANU), 36, 39–41
  and Zimbabwe African People's Union (ZAPU), 28, 88–92
Mugabe, Sally Hayfron, 24, 35, 40, 76
Mungoshi, Charles, 64, 76, 102
Mutare, 57, 102
Muzorewa, Abel, 44, 45, 46, 48, 94, 102

Namibia, 84
National Democratic Party (NDP), 25–27, 102
National parks, 81–82
Ndebele, 15–16, 17, 52, 75, 77, 86, 87–88, 89, 90, 95, 102
Nehanda, Mbuya, 33–34
Nhongo, Teurai Ropa, 78, 79
Nigeria, 26
Nkola, Enos, 39
Nkomo, Joshua, 22–23, 24, 25, 26–28, 33, 38, 41–43, 44, 46, 48, 88–95, 102
Nkrumah, Kwame, 23–24, 102
Nyerere, Julius, 28, 40, 41–42, 46, 102

O'Hea, Jerome, 20–21, 70
Operation Noah, 53

Parks, 81–82
Patriotic Front (PF), 42, 44, 46, 48, 50, 102
Pioneer Column, 15–16, 102
Population, 69, 76–77
Portugal, 37

Religion, 58
Reserves, 102
Rhodes, Cecil, 15, 16, 49, 56, 102
Rhodesia, 29, 30, 32–37, 41, 43–45, 71, 102. *See also* Southern Rhodesia; Zimbabwe
Rhodesian Front (RF), 28–29, 102

St. Paul's Mission, 43
Salisbury, 11, 13, 16, 17, 43, 44, 50, 54, 71, 103. *See also* Harare
Sandawana emeralds, 66
Sanitation, 72
"The Setting Sun and the Rolling World," 64

Shona, 13–15, 16, 17, 19, 50, 52, 75, 77, 86, 87–88, 95, 103
Simpson, Colin, 25
Sithole, Ndabaningi, 28, 35–36, 40, 44, 94, 103
Smith, David, 25
Smith, Ian, 28, 30, 36, 37–38, 40, 41, 43–44, 45, 46, 50, 90, 103
South Africa, 21, 36, 37–38, 41, 68–69, 89
Southern Rhodesia, 11, 13, 16, 17, 18, 20, 22, 24–29, 81
Southern Rhodesia African National Congress, 22, 24
Spirit mediums, 33–34, 58, 103
Spiritual life, 58
Sports, 55–56
Suburbs, 57

Takuwera, Leopold, 25, 28, 35, 103
Tangwena, 40
Tanzania, 26, 28, 33, 39–40, 43, 45, 103
Teachers, 75
Tekere, Edgar, 39
"The Ten Shillings," 76
Thatcher, Margaret, 45–46
Tobacco, 22, 62, 65, 66
Todd, Garfield, 23, 24
Tourism, 82

Unemployment, 69, 75–76
United Nations, 30, 73

Veld, 53–54, 103
Victoria, Queen, 53
Victoria Falls, 53
Vorster, John, 37, 41

Whitehead, Sir Edgar, 26
Wildlife. *See* Animals; specific animals
Women, 59, 71, 77–80
World Wildlife Fund, 84

Zambezi River, 52, 53, 83, 103
Zambia, 26, 32, 37–38, 45, 65, 103
ZANU. *See* Zimbabwe African National Union
ZAPU. *See* Zimbabwe African People's Union
Zimbabwe
  agriculture, 53–54, 62–65
  bush country, 57–60
  cities and suburbs, 54–57, 65
  climate, 53–54
  constitution, 46
  economy, 62, 68–69, 76
  education, 60, 69, 70, 73–75
  elections, 47–48, 50
  exports, 68–69
  health care, 69–72
  history, 13–19
  housing, 73
  imports, 67
  independence, 49, 50
  industry, 65–67
  origin of name, 13, 29
  physical characteristics, 52–53
  population, 69, 76–77
  religion, 58
  time line, 97–98
  village life, 59–60
  women in, 77–80
Zimbabwe African National Union (ZANU), 28, 31–41, 43, 44–45, 48, 50, 86–87, 88–89, 90–91, 93, 94, 103
Zimbabwe African People's Union (ZAPU), 27–28, 33, 37, 44, 88–89, 90–92, 103
Zimbabwe-Rhodesia, 44
Zimbabwe: The Wages of War, 89
Zurich (Switz.), 40

ABOUT THE AUTHOR

Richard Worth has written a number of books on current affairs, including works on the Middle East, eastern Europe, and the Third World. He wanted to write a book on Robert Mugabe and Zimbabwe to demonstrate that, in a part of the world where countries are often poorly governed, there exists at least one notable exception.